I0740952

THE ABANDONED CAR

Also by Stephanie Rosenbaum:

THE CLUE IN THE OLD RING
A Sandy Connors Mystery

Lucky Valley Press, 2013

THE ABANDONED CAR

A Sandy Connors Mystery

Stephanie Rosenbaum

LUCKY VALLEY PRESS

Carmel California

Cover by David Gordon

Book design by Lucky Valley Press

ISBN 978-0-9856655-7-9

Published by Lucky Valley Press
PO Box 5474, Carmel California 93921
www.luckyvalleypress.com

Printed in the United States of America

Twenty one year old Sandy Connors sat curled up in her favorite armchair, reading a book on Renaissance art. It was a blustery Thursday in February, and Sandy had lighted a fire. She was startled to hear the doorbell ring. "I wonder who that could be,"she asked aloud. Her father was at work and her mother was in Arizona, visiting her sister, Beatrice. Sandy herself did not expect any visitors and didn't remember her father saying he was expecting anyone. "Maybe it's Rose or Lily," Sandy thought of her two closest friends, sisters, who lived only a few blocks away. She put a bookmark in her book and stepped to the door.

Peeking through the peephole, Sandy was surprised to see a policeman on the doorstep! She opened the door and greeted the officer. He introduced himself as Officer Crowley. "I don't want to cause you any alarm, Ma'am," he began. "I'm here to ask about the white car parked across the street." He indicated a white station wagon, parked in front of the house directly across the street from the Connors'. "Does it belong to you or anyone in your family?"

"No." Sandy said. "I don't know to whom it belongs. It has been parked there for several days. I assumed it belonged to the Wright's guests." Sandy named the family that lived in the house. "Mr. Wright mentioned that his son's family was coming to visit this week." Officer Crowley nodded, and explained that it was Mr. Wright who called in a complaint about the car. "His family's visit was delayed and they are arriving this weekend. Mr. Wright complained that the station wagon is abandoned and is blocking the parking spot his son is to use. He would like the car towed by the weekend if the owner cannot be located."

"I see." Sandy asked, "Can the police run the information on the plates and use that to find the owner's name?"

"We've put a request in to the DMV." Officer Crowley said. "I came to answer Mr. Wright's complaint and thought I would speak to the neighbors before we have the car towed, in case someone who lives nearby parked it there. It's a slim chance; I agree with Mr. Wright, the car has likely been abandoned." Officer Crowley said if Sandy had no more information, he would continue to ask around the neighborhood. Sandy said she had nothing more to share and thanked the man for helping the elderly Wright couple with the complaint. After the officer left, she returned to the living room and again picked up her book, but could not focus.

"Why would someone abandon a car in this neighborhood?" she thought. "This is a very low traffic street so a strange car would be noticed." Perhaps the people who abandoned the car might be in some sort of trouble! "Oh, I hope the police are able to find out their names from the license information! Maybe I can help them!" She ruminated in this vein until she again heard the doorbell ring. Thinking it was Officer Crowley returning, she hastened to answer it, but it was her friends on the step, Rose and Lily Pinkerton. Rose Pinkerton was an eighteen year old art student, several years younger than her sister Lily, and Sandy, both twenty-one. After graduating from the local high school, Sandy and Lily had spent the past few years traveling and engaged in various volunteer projects in Santa Maria, where all three lived. The girls had been close friends for years and had recently solved a mystery revolving around an heirloom ring Mr. Pinkerton purchased which led the girls to the discovery of an old treasure.

"Hi!" Lily, the more outgoing and spunky of the sisters, said. "We were bored, cooped up inside in this terrible weather! So we decided to go outside and look where we wound up!" Sandy laughed as she noted the sisters' windblown appearance. All three trooped into the Connors' living room and Sandy threw a fresh log on the fire to dispel the chill that followed the sisters inside. "It is terrible out there!" Rose, a more retiring girl, added. She disliked the risky adventures that her older sister enjoyed. "Sandy? Hello?" Rose waved a hand in front of Sandy's face.

"Oh!" Sandy was jolted out of her reverie. "Sorry to drift off ... there's been an interesting happening here today. I guess I was thinking about it."

"Now, Sandy," Lily cautioned. "Are you sure you aren't making up clues out of thin air? I know you've been hankering for another mystery since we found that old treasure!" Sandy laughed and agreed that she enjoyed solving that mystery. "I would love another one to work on! Maybe I am overreacting. I'll tell you two what happened and you can judge!" She told the girls the story, starting with Mr. Wright's notice about his family's imminent visit. She pointed out the station wagon across the street and explained that it had not seemed suspicious to her because she was under the mistaken impression that Mr. Wright's son and his family were in town.

"But he's not?" Rose asked. "What happened to him?" Sandy hastened to assure her that nothing untoward had happened to Mr. Wright's son. "The visit was delayed, and, in fact, he and his family are arriving this weekend. Mr. Wright called in a complaint about an abandoned car in front of his house that was blocking his son's parking spot. He wants the station wagon moved or towed by this weekend." Lily said she was curious about who would abandon a car in this neighborhood. Sandy agreed and said that was why she thought it so strange. "Shortly before you girls arrived, a police officer came to ask if the car was mine or if I knew who owned it. The authorities are waiting to hear back from the DMV about the license plate information. I was just wondering who would choose a neighborhood like this to abandon a car, and thinking that perhaps the owner of the car needs help!"

"Sandy, you need a new hobby!" Rose interjected. "Even if the car was abandoned by someone who needs help, how could you possibly find them, or hope to help them even if you did find them?" Sandy agreed that she had nothing definite to go on but insisted that something didn't feel right. "Tomorrow I'm going to drop by the police station and see if they've discovered the owners' names. Perhaps they may tell me, since I worked with them on the last case, and I may be able to help trace them!" Sandy's eyes sparkled at the thought of a new mystery. Lily wished her friend luck and asked to be kept up to date about what she found out. Rose just shook her head, and soon the three were discussing plans for a summer trip.

Sandy could not get the abandoned car, or the thought that the owner was in trouble, out of her mind. When her father came home from his job at a nearby university, she discussed her thoughts with him. "Well, dear, you really don't have any evidence of foul play in this case. Then again, I've tried to teach you to always listen to your instincts. I agree, leaving a car in this neighborhood is strange. I first noticed it last Monday morning." Sandy thought about it, and then agreed.

"And, Dad, it had to have been left sometime in the very early morning! I took mother to the airport Sunday night and didn't get home until just after midnight. I'm certain the station wagon wasn't parked on the street then!" Mr. Connors conceded that leaving a car late at night did seem suspicious, but he pointed out that the car was very well parked and showed no signs of denting or scratching to indicate there had been an accident. "Perhaps it broke down?" He suggested.

"That would explain the lack of dents. But, Dad, that doesn't make sense." Sandy countered. "It's not a very old car. Unless someone was very wealthy they wouldn't leave a car in that condition there. Certainly a mechanics shop could repair any engine problems and it would be worth something to take the car to a body shop. No, Dad, the more I think about it the more I'm convinced that there's something wrong about the car being left there! Maybe it was stolen," Sandy mused. Her father said that if that were the case, the license information would certainly tell the police that and they would soon impound it. "Either way, I'm sure it will soon be towed off the street."

Sandy agreed, but claimed she was still going to stop by the station tomorrow to talk to an officer about what they had discovered. "If that car belongs to someone who is in trouble, I'm going to help them!" Sandy stated.

CHAPTER 2

The next morning Sandy was up early. She ate breakfast with her father, who had several meetings that day and probably would not be home until late in the evening. Sandy reminded her father that she was going to go to the police station to ask some questions about the white station wagon. She peeked out the window and saw that it was still there. "I may go over and look at the car itself and see if there are any clues!" she said, commenting that the weather seemed much nicer today. Her father reminded her that she could be overreacting to the car. "Perhaps the people left it because it is broken down or they have a second car they like better."

"Dad, I don't think that's it. It just seems wrong, somehow." Mr. Connors chuckled, and let the matter drop. Soon he was on his way to work and Sandy was crossing the street to look at the abandoned car. She brought a notebook and a magnifying glass with her. "I can't open the car doors," Sandy said to herself, knowing that was illegal. "But I can peek in any windows that aren't tinted. Perhaps, if there is anything in the car, it will give me a clue to the owner!" Sandy was delighted to see that several of the windows were not colored. Looking inside, she gasped. The backseat of the car was covered in baby bottles and toys!

"There was a child in this car!" Sandy was aghast. She knew this changed the matter. "If there's a child in trouble then it's even more important that I find them!" She was sorely tempted to try one of the doors, but she knew she shouldn't. "I will ask the police to open the doors and examine the things inside," she determined. She knew that if the authorities opened the car after towing it, that it would be legal. She continued to look around the car but saw nothing else that gave her any clues. She noted the license number of the car, and saw that there were no dents or scratches. "I guess that means it was left here on purpose. I can't imagine why!" Now deeply concerned, Sandy was just about to return to her house when Mr. Wright opened his front door.

"Sandy! Good morning!" the friendly older gentleman said. "I don't suppose you know whose car that is?" Sandy said she did not, but explained that a police officer had spoken to her yesterday and she thought they were planning to tow it if they couldn't find the owners by the weekend. "I thought perhaps there might be some clues inside the car, so I came over to take a look."

"Always looking for somebody to help!" Mr. Wright chuckled. "I hope they find the owners; normally I wouldn't mind leaving the car for them, whenever they come back, but my son is coming in to town and where else can he park? He's bringing my newest grandchild," the old man grinned fondly, "who's only two months old. I don't want him having to walk blocks and blocks with the baby and boxes and bags!" Sandy agreed. She knew that Mr. Wright and his wife were both slightly infirm and neither of them would be able to walk that far.

"I'm going to stop by the police station today and ask them about the car." Sandy said. "If you would like, I'll come by and tell you what they say." Mr. Wright said he would appreciate that. "I'm not trying to be a nuisance," the old man said, "It's just bad timing that the car is out there right now!" Sandy said she understood and would be back shortly with news for him. The girl then recrossed the street and drove her own car downtown to the police station. After parking, she entered and asked to speak to Officer Crowley. Fortunately, the policeman was at the station and the two were shown into a meeting room to talk. Sandy explained why she was especially interested in the car and shared her recent discoveries. "I'm worried that there may be a child who needs help somewhere!" She stated grimly.

"I agree this changes the matter," Officer Crowley said. "The information on the license plate is expected at any moment now, hopefully the name will provide us with a clue. If you would like to wait, I'm sure we'll be getting a call any minute." Sandy thanked the man and said she would step into the reception area of the station to await the news. She had barely started towards the door when the receptionist opened the door and said she had received the names from the DMV. "Peter and Betty Mullens are listed as the owners of the vehicle," the young woman said. "Address listed as 324 16th Avenue, Santa Maria. The car was registered 18 months ago, and has had no major accidents or liabilities listed at any point." Officer Crowley thanked the woman for the information, and she returned to the front desk.

Sandy was intrigued by the information. She knew that the car was a new model, only a year or two old. "The Mullens must have purchased the car new," she mused out loud, mentioning that perhaps she could find the lot where it had been purchased and ask the salesman there some questions. Officer Crowley agreed that the car was a new model and said her idea was a good one. "I'm going to look up the Mullens family in our files. It seems to me that I remember hearing that name before, in connection with an arrest warrant. Perhaps it's a different Mullens, however. Please stay here for just a moment while I find the book." Sandy agreed to wait, and spent the time mulling over why a family would abandon a new car. "I'm convinced there's been trouble- such a new model, with no reported accidents, would be worth a fair amount of money! Abandoning it makes no sense!"

Officer Crowley was back shortly, carrying the book. Accompanying him was an officer with whom Sandy had worked on the mystery surrounding the stolen ring, Officer Murray. Sandy greeted him and asked if he was working on the abandoned car case, too. He looked grim, and said that the case was much more than an abandoned car. He took the book Officer Crowley carried and flipped several pages, then pointed to a notation about an arrest warrant. Sandy gasped! The notation read, "Betty Mullens, wanted in connection with the kidnapping of a six month old girl named Lisa."

"Kidnapping!" Sandy was shocked, "How terrible!" Both officers agreed, and said that this added a new urgency to the case. "So far our men have been unable to trace Betty Mullens. This is our first definite clue since the kidnapping was reported two days ago." Sandy asked for more details about what had happened and the child that was missing. "Lisa, a six

month old girl, was taken from her foster home last
Tuesday evening. She had been surrendered to the
Santa Maria hospital when she was only a few days
old. She was left with no note or identifying papers
at all. Lisa was taken to the Santa Maria Home for
Children - a private orphanage - after nurses at the
hospital found her to be in good health. She stayed
for three weeks in the Home, then a foster family was
found for her. The foster parents, Richard and Maria
Webber, have worked with the Home for many years
and have fostered many children. Everyone with
whom they work says wonderful things about them.
Lisa lived with the Webbers for almost five months,
and then was taken last week. Maria Webber reported
that she had just put the child down for her afternoon
nap and had gone into the kitchen to prepare supper.
The child reportedly was a deep sleeper and Mrs.
Webber rarely had trouble getting her to take a
nap. One hour later, Mrs. Webber went into the
child's room to check on her and found that she was
gone! She called the police immediately, and it was
determined that the kidnapper had crept in through
the back door and taken the child. Investigations
are still ongoing as to how the assailant entered the
child's bedroom, which Mrs. Webber locked each day
while she napped. Additionally, Mrs. Webber had a
baby monitor in use, which was tampered with before
the kidnapping took place.

"The only suspect Mrs. Webber could think of was
Betty Mullens, who worked as a part time cleaning
woman and seemed very interested in the child. Mrs.
Mullens was supposed to come Wednesday to clean
for the Webbers but did not show up. Mrs. Webber

said she had no contact information for Mrs. Mullens.
We're investigating that aspect as well." Sandy was
shocked. Kidnapping was a serious crime, she knew.
She wondered what could drive Betty Mullens to
kidnap a child.

CHAPTER 3

"Sandy," Officer Murray said, interrupting her reverie, "We would be glad of your help with this case. Since you've worked with the force before we feel you can be trusted. If you discover anything more, please let us know." Sandy assured the man she would, and said she would like to speak with the Webbers, the matron in charge of the Home where the child spent a short period of time and several other people who might have information. "I'm sure the police will be towing the car and examining the contents." Officer Murray answered in the affirmative. "May I ask to be informed of any discoveries?" Again the officer assured her it would be so. Sandy then bade the officers goodbye, promising to tell them anything she discovered about the case.

Sandy considered where she should best begin investigating this case. She thought about driving directly to the Webbers' home to speak to Mrs. Webber, or going to the private orphanage where the girl was housed for a short while. "Or perhaps I should start at the Santa Maria hospital, where the child was first dropped off. I can follow the trail from there," Sandy thought out loud. After deciding that this would be the wisest course of action, she turned her vehicle in the direction of the hospital. She knew that records were kept confidential but she hoped that perhaps there would be someone there who could give her even a small clue about the kidnapping. "I find it odd that Mrs. Mullens would choose to kidnap her employer's foster child, rather than trying to adopt or foster a child of her own. If she is that thoughtless

then the child is surely in danger, but if she had a
special reason for wanting this child then perhaps this
isn't a simple kidnapping case," Sandy mused.

Soon she reached the Santa Maria hospital and
parked her car in an open space. The wind was still
fierce and she struggled to reach the hospital door.
"I hope there are no bad accidents today," Sandy
thought to herself, "the wind is so strong!" She was
glad to note that the hospital did not seem especially
busy and that the reception area was empty. This
pleased her, as Sandy preferred a private interview
with the young woman at the reception desk. Sandy
approached and introduced herself. She told the
woman briefly about her mission and asked if anyone
would be able to help her. The receptionist thought for
a moment, and then said that she would call one of
the hospital administrators. "The cases where children
are surrendered here are kept confidential, but
since this child has been kidnapped, it is a different
matter. Perhaps Mr. Rogers will be able to help you."
The woman put in the call and presently Sandy was
shown into the office of one of the men who worked
on the hospital's policy and public relations. Again,
Sandy explained her mission.

"I see," Mr. Rogers said when he had heard
Sandy's entire story. "As I'm sure you're aware, the
surrendered children and any information about their
families is kept confidential. In this case, however,
there is no information whatsoever. After reading the
police report I looked up Lisa's records and there is no
information there at all. I am at liberty to say that the
child was found outside a back door at around 2 AM,
last September. This door has a bell since it cannot
be opened from the outside. This bell rings at one of

the nurses' stations down the hall. Usually the door
is used only for scheduled deliveries so it is unlocked
and the bell is rarely used. The nurse on duty - if you
would like you can speak with her as well - heard
it ring and went to answer it when she finished the
report on which she was working. She said it was
about five minutes after the ring that she answered.
She was surprised to find a small baby, well wrapped
up, and in good health. She was sleeping. There was
no note, but the nurses all know about the child
surrender policy so she assumed this was the case.
She took the child in to the baby unit and gave her
over to the care of the charge nurse there. From then
on the files on baby Lisa would be in the baby unit,
but I know that she was found to be in good health.

"We keep all surrendered children one week, in
case the mother changes her mind, or some other
family member comes for them and can prove a
relationship. Then we give the children to one of the
various Homes and Orphanages with which we work.
Lisa went to the Santa Maria Home for Children,
which is only six blocks away. That's all I know about
the case," Mr. Rogers said. "Would you like to speak
to the nurse that found Lisa?" Sandy said she would
and was pointed to the recovery wing of the hospital.
"The nurse's name is Amanda. She's on duty now, and
if you speak with whomever is at the nurse's station
inside the wing, a message will get to her. She may
have to finish rounds before she is free to speak with
you," Mr. Rogers cautioned. Sandy assured the man
she understood and would be patient, thanked him
for his help and left to find the recovery wing.

Sandy found the wing easily enough and spoke
to the woman at the nurse's station. "I'm looking for

Amanda," Sandy said, "I have a few questions about a surrendered child that she found in September." The woman looked surprised, but smiled as she answered, "I'm Amanda. Amanda White. How can I help you?" Amanda was a woman in her fifties, Sandy guessed and seemed friendly and competent. Sandy explained why she was asking and said that any information Amanda had would be helpful. "I do remember the child you're asking about," Amanda said. "There are very few surrendered in Santa Maria, and hardly anyone uses the back door, so I remember it ringing. I was here, working on a report when the buzzer went and the light lit up." Amanda pointed to a light on a large panel that was marked "Door #3." "I don't ever remember it ringing before, or since. It's a delivery entrance, and takes scheduled deliveries, you see, so we always know when someone will be using it and unlock it before they come," the nurse explained. "Since I was in the middle of a report, I finished it, then went to see who was there. There was one other nurse on duty in the wing that night and she was busy with patients the whole time so she only heard about it after I told her when our shift was over.

"I went to answer the door and to my surprise there was no one there! There was a bundle of blankets placed on the ground. I didn't even know it was a child, at first; it was so well wrapped up. I picked it up and then realized it was a baby. I immediately assumed it was a surrendered child. To be honest I was so concerned about the baby that I didn't even look for anyone around who might be the mother. I took the baby inside and out here to the station. I had been informed of the protocol when I first started working here twenty years ago but had never actually

been the one to find a surrendered child. I called up
to the baby wing and one of the nurses from there
came and took the girl - Nurse Wright, I think it was.
That was the last I saw of her. I did speak with the
nurse from the baby wing later and find out that it was
a little girl, in very good health. She was about three
days old, apparently. I guess no one came back to
claim her, because she was sent to an orphanage after
a week passed. I never heard anything about her after
that - but, imagine, the little baby I found on the step,
kidnapped!"

Sandy thanked Amanda for her help and said she
would be sure to tell her if baby Lisa were found.
Then she proceeded up to the baby unit, hoping to
speak to Nurse Wright. She met with disappointment,
however. The young woman at the nurse's station
informed her that Nurse Wright had retired almost
four months ago. "She moved to Florida to be near
her family," the woman said. "If you want I can get
you a mailing address where she said a letter would
reach her." Sandy thanked the woman and waited
while she found it. "This is actually her family's
address. Shelly - Nurse Wright, that is - didn't know
where exactly she was going to live yet so she didn't
have a personal address or phone number." Sandy
thanked the woman and left, wondering if Nurse
Wright would have enough information to make
sending her a letter worthwhile.

Sandy was unable to think of anyone else at the
hospital who would be able to help her, so she left.
Seeing that it was nearing lunchtime, Sandy drove
home. "I'll call Rose and Lily and invite them to
have lunch with me. I can tell them about the new
mystery, then perhaps this afternoon the three of us

can go and speak with the matron at the Home."
Soon the two girls were on the way over to Sandy's
house, both declaring they were eager to hear about
the new developments. Sandy prepared soup and
sandwiches and set the table while she waited.
Presently the doorbell rang and she let the sisters in.
After exchanging greetings, the three proceeded into
the dining room. No sooner had the three served
themselves soup and sat down when Lily asked,
excitedly, "What's going on, Sandy? You say there's a
new mystery?"

CHAPTER 4

Sandy laughed and said that there was a new mystery. "You know the abandoned car, across the street? The one I was telling you about yesterday? Well, I went over and looked at it this morning and it's full of baby clothes!" The Pinkerton sisters gasped. "I went to the police station and was informed that the car is registered to Peter and Betty Mullens. Girls, Betty Mullens is wanted on a charge of kidnapping a six month old baby!" Again, the sisters gasped. Rose was aghast, "Do you think she took the kidnapped child in that vehicle?" Sandy said she feared that was the case. "The baby girl was reported missing last Thursday, the car was abandoned here Monday. This morning I spoke with Officer Murray - he's in charge of the kidnapping case - and he said if I wanted to help investigate I could."

"And I bet you've already interviewed half a dozen people about the case, and know exactly where the baby girl is!" Rose joked.

"Not quite," Sandy said, smiling. "I went to the Santa Maria General Hospital where the girl was surrendered."

"Surrendered?" Lily said, "I thought she was kidnapped!"

"Oh, of course!" Sandy said, feeling foolish, "let me start at the beginning. Nearly six months ago, Baby Lisa was surrendered at the Santa Maria hospital. Are you two familiar with that law?" Rose shook her head. "I've heard of it, but I don't know what it is, really," she admitted. Lily said she also did not understand the details and urged Sandy to explain.

"Essentially, this law allows any woman to leave her child at any hospital or police station in the state of California within the first week of the child's life with no consequences. It is called 'surrendering.' Apparently many women who take advantage of this law do so because they fear they will not be able to adequately care for the child. This is sometimes done anonymously, as was the case with Lisa. Anyway, a nurse at the Santa Maria General Hospital found Lisa at 2 AM about six months ago. No name or information was found with her. As is the case with surrendered children, she was taken to the baby wing where she was examined. Lisa was found to be healthy, and after one week had passed she was given to the Santa Maria Home for Children - a local private orphanage - where she lived for about three weeks. Then, Richard and Maria Webber, a local couple who apparently have fostered several children, took her. Several weeks later, Betty Mullens began working as a housekeeper for the Webbers. She is the only suspect in the kidnapping, which occurred last Thursday. Maria Webber reported putting Lisa down for her nap, locking the bedroom door- as she apparently did every afternoon- and going to cook dinner. She had a baby monitor turned on Lisa room, which either did not work or Lisa didn't cry. One hour later, Mrs. Webber came to check on Lisa and found her gone. Betty Mullens did not arrive to work the next day and is wanted for kidnapping.

"Now this car is found, which is apparently in good working condition and full of children's clothes and toys and registered to Betty Mullens and Peter

Mullens, presumably her husband. The police are going to tow it tomorrow and examine it. I'm sure if anything comes to light, Officer Murray will phone me. I went to the hospital this morning and spoke with the woman who found Lisa, but she had nothing new to add to the story. The nurse who took care of Lisa in the baby wing retired and moved to Florida four months ago. I have an address for her family and I'll write this evening, in case she has anything to add. I'd like to speak with the Matron at the Santa Maria Home for Children, and the Webbers as well. I also want to try and trace the vehicle - it's a new model that the Mullens registered eighteen months ago, so I'm betting they bought it new - and try and speak with the car salesman, if I can. Are you girls interested in helping out?" Sandy finished her narration with a smile.

"Jiminy Cricket, Sandy!" Lily exclaimed, "You certainly don't waste any time! Of course we want to help! That poor baby may be in danger!" Rose agreed she wanted to help, too. "There are a few things I don't understand, though." Rose said. "Why would the Mullens abandon their car? Surely they must know the registration can be traced! And why kidnap a six-month-old foster girl? If Betty Mullens wants a child so badly, she can legally adopt." Sandy agreed that certain aspects of the case puzzled her so far. "Of course, we don't know the entire story yet. I think the Mullens were either forced to abandon the car for some reason, which adds an entirely new dimension and would explain why they left so many baby things inside, or Betty Mullens may not be altogether sane. That's one of the primary things I want to talk to the Webbers about. If Betty Mullens is ill, that would explain the illogical kidnapping, and the abandoned car. I also want to ask about how she came to be hired as their housekeeper. Officer Murray said that Mrs. Webber claimed not to have any contact information for Betty Mullens, which is curious."

"Sandy, what about Peter Mullens, her supposed husband?" Lily asked. "What part does he play here?" Sandy said she didn't know, and admitted he had slipped her mind. "I intend to call the police tomorrow and speak with Officer Murray about the car. I'll ask him to look up Peter Mullens and see what he does. He might not be involved with the kidnapping; perhaps he's in trouble too!" Sandy mused. Lily agreed that if his wife is mentally ill, he might be in need of help. Rose chimed in, "Perhaps he knows where his wife and the baby girl are but is afraid to turn her in because he doesn't want to get his wife in trouble."

"That would make him an accessory to the kidnapping," Sandy said. "Whatever his story is, he's someone we should try to find as well. I will make a note to ask Officer Murray about that tomorrow. In the meantime, do you two want to come with me to the Home for Children? It's only a few blocks from the hospital, and the Matron or one of the workers there may have some useful information for us. I do hope they remember baby Lisa!" Both sisters said they were eager to begin working on the mystery and would like to go to the Home with Sandy. Soon the three were in Sandy's car as she drove downtown. The Santa Maria Home for Children proved to be easy to find, and was located on a spacious green plot of land. Sandy parked near the front walkway and the three stepped into the wind to walk up to the door.

Sandy admired the trees and flowers as the girls
walked, and said she hoped the children in the
home were able to spend time outside. The girls had
passed through a wrought iron gate in the fence,
which encircled the property. Lily agreed that the
grounds were beautiful, but said the wind would
surely blow the little children away! She made a
show of struggling against the wind and pretended to
be blown backwards, wind milling her arms as she
feigned losing her balance. Sandy and Rose laughed,
and the three girls were in gay spirits by the time they
reached the front door of the building.

CHAPTER 5

The lobby of the Santa Maria Home for Children was brightly lit and comfortable. Sandy saw a sign-in sheet near a bell. She wrote her own name on the sheet and rang the bell before passing the pen to Rose and Lily. Soon a middle-aged woman with a pleasant smile stepped in to the room. "How can I help you girls today?" She asked. Sandy stepped forward and introduced herself. "I was hoping to speak with the matron for just a few minutes." The woman, who said her name was Joanne, asked the girls to wait just a moment. "Mrs. Carpenter, our matron, frequently has phone meetings with potential foster parents or people looking to adopt. If she is on the phone, I'll have to ask you to wait." Sandy assured Joanne that the girls did not mind waiting. Joanne went to see Mrs. Carpenter.

As it turned out, the Matron was on the phone. "I'm sorry," Joanne said, "Mrs. Carpenter is doing an interview of potential foster parents. These interviews typically take about half an hour. Is that too long to wait?" Sandy was secretly pleased by the wait. She assured Joanne that it was not too long at all. "Could we perhaps walk around the grounds while we wait?" Sandy asked.

"I can give you a tour," Joanne offered. "Due to safety regulations, any guests must be accompanied by a staff member at all times," she explained. Sandy thanked Joanne for the offer and said she would be interested in seeing the Home. Rose and Lily said they would like to come, too, and soon the four were walking down the hallway towards the dormitories.

"We have between fifty and sixty children here,
ranging from infants to age ten. These rooms are for
the older children, eight to ten." Joanne gestured
down a side hallway where the girls saw many doors.
The walls were decorated with handmade artwork.

"I presume these pieces were done by the
children?" Rose asked, pointing to several childlike
paintings on the walls.

"Yes," Joanne said. "All the school-aged children
attend Santa Maria elementary, down the road.
Frequently the children do art projects at school and
bring them back here. They also do art Mondays and
Thursdays after school before dinner. You see, we set
up organized activities for the children after school
and on weekends. Mondays and Thursdays are art,
Tuesdays are for music and Wednesdays and Fridays
it's sports. The children have three meals a day either
packed into lunch boxes or in the cafeteria. We'll go
there next," Joanne said, steering the girls towards a
door at the end of the hall. The three stepped out into
the blustery air and crossed a small patio. "When it's
nice outside the children can eat out here, or read or
play during free time, which is every day after dinner
and weekend afternoons."

"What do the children do on weekends?" Sandy
asked.

"That changes weekend to weekend," Joanne
smiled. "We have books and art supplies they can use
in the afternoon. We show films at night, after dinner.
In the morning we have some wonderful volunteers
who take small groups of children to local museums or
to the stores for shopping. Any doctor's visits are taken
care of on the weekend. Of course, we have a nurse
on staff but sometimes the children become sick or

get hurt, or need to visit a dentist. On Sunday morning
the children that want to can accompany some of
the staff members to church. The younger children,
of course, are watched by staff members all the time,
but even the babies get taken out to the gardens in the
summertime." The four had now reached the door to
the cafeteria, which Joanne opened.

The cafeteria was a large open room with round
tables. Sandy saw a buffet set up along one wall.
Joanne said she worked in the kitchens most of the
time. "We have a large kitchen staff, and we cook all
the food on site here. We try to provide the children
with healthy meals." She smiled.

"What about the children who are given to foster
parents?" Sandy asked.

"That's not my area of expertise," Joanne said,
"But I do know that we have more children sent
here than we can take, unfortunately, so some of
them are given to certain couples that have been
chosen as foster parents. Mrs. Carpenter takes care of
interviewing them all, and I know she's very careful
about which couples are chosen. She can tell you
more about that, and about which kids are selected
for foster care. I just take care of getting the ones that
stay here to eat their vegetables; that's all one person
can handle!" Joanne laughed, as did Sandy and the
Pinkerton sisters. The four toured the gymnasium and
another dormitory before Joanne said she thought
Mrs. Carpenter would be almost done with her phone
interview. "Let me take you back to the reception area
and check, then I'll need to get back to work." The
four returned, and fortunately the matron was finished
with her phone call. Joanne introduced the three girls
then excused herself.

"Hello, Mrs. Carpenter. Thank you so much for speaking with us," Sandy shook hands with the Matron. Rose and Lily followed suit. Mrs. Carpenter was a gray-haired woman, neatly dressed in a pressed black suit. She looked eminently capable and Sandy hoped she would have some information about Lisa. Quickly, Sandy explained why the girls were there. "I'm working in cooperation with the Santa Maria police department on a kidnapping case - the child involved stayed here for several weeks before being given to the Webbers for foster care. Lisa was her name."

Mrs. Carpenter's face turned grave. "I remember baby Lisa. She was younger than we usually give to foster families, but she was a very well behaved, quiet baby. And the Webbers have been fostering for us for almost twenty years now. They are one of our most responsible and careful foster families." Sandy asked the woman to tell her about Lisa's time at the Home. "Well, she came to us in the same manner as many of the very young children. Any baby surrendered at a local hospital or police station is sent to one of the local orphanages or homes after one week has passed. I don't know the exact number of children that are surrendered - it's kept confidential, I'm told - but I can tell you that we get two or three surrendered babies a year. They're quite young, and often have long-term health problems. Some mothers, I imagine, have a child and when they discover it will need expensive and possibly life-long health care they realize they lack the funds to take care of the child's special needs and surrender the child. I would guess that nearly ninety percent of babies who are surrendered and then brought to us have special medical needs. We, of course, have the staff and funding to take care of these children.

"But baby Lisa, she was healthy. She was very engaged, quiet and calm for such a young child. When you see so many children grow up you learn to recognize early signs, so I can be confident when I say Lisa will be a very smart woman once she's grown. Because she was so well behaved, we were able to give her to foster care sooner than normal. You see, we have fifty-nine children in residence currently, and the most we can have is sixty. So we were looking for children who would do well in a foster situation, matched with suitable foster families. As I said, the Webbers have long been one of our most reliable families. They were happy to take Lisa, even though she was younger than any other children they had previously fostered. Before a child is given to a foster family we do a home tour - even if they've fostered for us before - and the family and the child meet at the Home, then again at the foster parent's house before the child is given over to the foster family's care. These steps were followed in Lisa's case and there were no issues found. I heard that there was a question about why the baby monitor didn't alert Mrs. Webber to the kidnapping while it was in progress; we're awaiting a police report, but I personally feel sure that Maria Webber would never leave a child alone without a working monitor and believe the police will find evidence of tampering. Beyond that, I feel the Webbers are victims of circumstance and are not to blame. Here at the Home, we will do everything we can to cooperate with the police in this investigation." The woman finished her narrative.

"Mrs. Carpenter, can you tell me a little bit about how the foster families are chosen, please?" Sandy asked.

"Certainly, dear. We advertise in the local papers and provide contact information for the Home. Interested families approach us. We set up a phone interview, then an interview in-person. I conduct all the phone interviews and the in-person interviews are conducted by myself and a team of other staff members, at least four at each interview. We speak to the couple together, then to each person privately. A packet of documentation is requested for the in-person interview, including proof of insurance, personal references and medical history. If the interviews are satisfactory, we run a background check on all involved parties. If that brings up nothing suspicious, we begin a series of house visits. We schedule two on different days and perform two unscheduled visits. We sometimes visit the potential foster family members' places of work as well, if it seems necessary. If the family has any pets we ask for proof of vaccinations and basic obedience training. We check on the validity of the provided documentation and call one or two of the references for each potential family. If the family has biological or adopted children we speak with them as well. Some families that serve as foster parents for other organizations nearby show interest in working with us as well, but laws prevent families from working as foster parents for more than one organization.

"Before a child is placed with the family - and this process occurs for each child placed - we again visit the home of the family and do the meetings between the family and the child, as I already explained. Once a child is placed, someone on staff visits the home within a week, then again at the end of the first month and once a month thereafter for the first year. If there are no problems within that year then the visits taper to once every six months and that schedule continues for as long as the child remains with the parents."

"That's a very rigorous and thorough program!" Lily commented. "You say the Webbers have been working with you for twenty years?"

"That is correct," Mrs. Carpenter said. "They have been through every step of the process and not once has there been as issue. They are very responsible, organized and upright people. Despite this unfortunate occurrence, I feel sure that we will be able to call on them as foster parents again and it will all be satisfactorily worked out. Is there anything else you wish to ask?" Mrs. Carpenter smiled kindly. Sandy, knowing how busy the woman must be, thanked her for her time and for the information and the three girls soon left the woman's office. Noting that it was nearing dinner time, Sandy drove the Pinkerton sisters back to their house. She promised to call them in the morning before she did anymore work on the mystery. Sandy then turned her car toward her own house.

At home that evening, Sandy began to prepare dinner for herself and her father. "It will be nice when Mother gets back, day after tomorrow," Sandy thought, missing the laughter and conversation she and her mother enjoyed in the kitchen. But the young sleuth enjoyed cooking, and soon had a pan of water boiling and a sauce simmering. "I'll broil some chicken," she thought, "and toss a salad. Dad will be home quite soon, I'm sure." True to her guess, at that moment she heard the garage door opening and soon her father arrived. He kissed his daughter and offered to set the table while she finished cooking. Soon the two were seated for their evening meal. Sandy began to tell her father about what she had discovered that day.

"Dad, the abandoned car across the street? It's led me to a kidnapping case!" Sandy gave her father a summary of the information in the case. She shared what she learned at the hospital and the Home earlier in the day. Mr. Connors listened carefully, and said he was proud of Sandy for following her intuition and alerting the police to the clue. "I expect you will continue working on this mystery and soon have several other good clues for them, too!" Sandy said she planned to phone the police in the morning. "I want to know if anything came to light when they examined the car. I will also ask if they can trace Peter Mullens. Lily noted that perhaps he isn't involved, or that he might be in need of help, too." Sandy shared her worry that Betty Mullens might be unstable. "That could mean that both her husband and the child are in danger!" Mr. Connors agreed, and cautioned his daughter against getting involved with the woman if she were found to be dangerous.

Sandy assured her father that she would be careful, but said that she needed to continue her investigation. "There are still so many unanswered questions! Was Lisa targeted as a kidnapping victim? If so, why? Why did the Mullens abandon their car? Are they in some kind of danger?" Mr. Connors agreed that those were all pertinent questions. "One thing I wonder, though, is how Betty Mullens came to be employed as a housekeeper. There's something odd about her employer not having her contact information," he mused. Sandy agreed that she thought that was strange as well. "It's something I intend to ask Maria Webber tomorrow when I speak with her. She must be very upset - I imagine she's taking the kidnapping very personally."

"It would be hard not to blame oneself, if a child under one's care was taken." Mr. Connors commented. Sandy explained about the baby monitor, and said that she also agreed that the kidnapper had probably tampered with it. "That's one more thing I must ask the police when I phone them tomorrow."

"Perhaps you should make a list!" Her father teased. "It would quite a long one!" Sandy smiled, and agreed that she did have many questions. "But, Dad," she said, "A young child may be in danger! It's important that I work on this case as quickly as I can, even if that means asking the police a lot of questions all at the same time!" Her father sobered and agreed that time was of the essence. Sandy then asked him about his day, and the two discussed his university classes while they finished their dinner. After they ate, the dishes were tidied up in short order. Mr. Connors went to his study to correct some papers his students had written while Sandy watched the evening news broadcast. The broadcast featured a short piece about a former bank robber who died while in prison. The robber had been part of a large gang, of which several members were still unaccounted for. Sandy shook her head, "Why is it that some people choose to turn their efforts toward evil?" she wondered. She was momentarily glad that her father had not watched the broadcast with her, for he would surely be teasing her about catching the robbers still on the loose! Still grinning, Sandy went upstairs to her room and read several more chapters in her art history book before turning out her light.

The next morning, Sandy was up early. She breakfasted with her father, and then phoned the Pinkertons. Rose answered, and asked excitedly what was going on with the case. Sandy said she planned to phone the police to ask about the car and Peter Mullens. "It looks a lot nicer outside today; why don't you and Lily get ready and come on over? I should be off the phone by the time you two get here." Rose agreed, and said they would be over in half an hour. As soon as Sandy had rung off, she dialed the Santa Maria police station. After identifying herself, she asked to be put through to Officer Murray or Officer Crowley. The receptionist told Sandy that Officer Murray was not on duty at that moment and put her through to Officer Crowley. The young policeman answered the phone after a few rings and, after she identified herself, Sandy asked him what the search of the car had found.

"Nothing very definite, I'm afraid," The officer admitted. "The baby clothes that were found were quite new; Maria Webber could not identify any of them so if Betty Mullens did take Lisa she bought new clothes for her. Mrs. Webber did say they were the same size as the clothes Lisa was wearing when she was kidnapped. The toys were also new. The car itself is in perfect condition. The gas tank was nearly empty, but there was a station near enough to reach easily before it ran out."

"Perhaps Betty Mullens had no way of filling the tank that couldn't be traced back to her," Sandy suggested. Officer Crowley said the thought had occurred to him as well. "We've put out an all points bulletin for Mrs. Mullens, using the description Maria Webber gave us. There was nothing else of interest about the car. It was, indeed, quite a new model. All documentation in the car had been taken." Sandy said that all this evidence pointed to the conclusion that the car had been deliberately but hurriedly abandoned. The officer agreed that was the most likely scenario. Sandy asked if any steps could be taken to attempt to track Peter Mullens. She shared her idea that he might not be involved in the kidnapping. "It's possible that Betty Mullens is slightly unbalanced, and Peter Mullens might be in need of help."

"We hadn't thought of that angle. I will have an officer begin to look for him immediately," Officer Crowley promised. "Preliminary searches for Betty Mullens in local and state records have turned up nothing other than the car registration. The address given on the registration is under surveillance but seems abandoned - it's very run down and looks like

no one has been there for several months, at least."
This was intriguing to Sandy - it indicated that the
address was a deliberate fake, given almost eighteen
months ago, or that the couple had abandoned the
apartment only a few months prior. She shared these
thoughts with the officer. "There's a very important
link we're missing, certainly," he agreed. "The Mullens
could be running from someone or they could be
professional cons, or perhaps one or both of them is
mentally ill. I think the faster we find them, the better
it will be for them as well as for baby Lisa," Crowley
said grimly.

Sandy said she agreed, and hoped that the Mullens
and Lisa were not in any danger. "If you find anything
about Peter Mullens, please let me know. I will be
going to speak with Mrs. Webber this morning. I want
to ask her about how Betty Mullens came to be in
her employ, and a few other things," Sandy said. The
officer wished her the best of luck, and assured her
that any information he received he would pass on
to her. Sandy hung up the phone and went into the
living room to wait for the Pinkertons to arrive.

CHAPTER 7

She did not have long to wait; Sandy had just had time to browse the front page of the daily paper when she heard the doorbell ring. She opened the door and let the two girls inside. The three gathered in the living room while Sandy explained what the police had found in the car. "Unfortunately, not much of any use," she said. "The baby clothes can't be traced to the Webbers; they're all new. So are the toys. If Betty Mullens kidnapped Lisa, she didn't take any of her belongings. There were no other baby accouterments in the car - no diapers, bottles or formula."

"That seems strange to me," Lily interjected. "If there was a young child in the car for any length of time surely there would be a need for diapers and formula!" Sandy agreed, and said she felt sure that the car had been abandoned on purpose and some things had been taken before the Mullens fled - including any diapers and Lisa's food. "If that's the case," Rose spoke up, "It would seem the Betty Mullens is taking care of Lisa. Maybe the child isn't in any danger at all!" Sandy said she didn't know. "But I have a hunch that both the Mullens and Lisa are in danger. I'm going to do all I can to help the police find them before anything can go wrong!"

Rose and Lily both agreed and said they wanted to help as well. Sandy outlined her plan to the girls. "Today, I think we should speak to Mrs. Webber. She must have some information on the type of person Betty Mullens is, which could be very useful. Tomorrow I have to go to the airport to pick up my mother. If the two of you want to continue with the

investigation I think you should go to the department
stores in town and speak with the clerks in the baby
departments. See if you can find out where Betty
Mullens bought the clothes and get any clues from the
clerks. She may have mentioned where she was going
or may have spoken about the child when she bought
the things." Rose and Lily agreed that they would
be happy to take care of that while Sandy was at the
airport.

"I'm glad!" Sandy said, "Thank you two so much.
Now, let's go and speak with Mrs. Webber!" The
three girls got into Sandy's car and soon were driving
to the Webbers' address. "The couple live in a nice
neighborhood, only a few minutes drive from the
downtown area," Sandy said. "I believe most of these
houses are quite expensive. The Webbers must be
well to do."

"I would imagine most of the foster families
that work with the Home are fairly wealthy," Rose
commented. "I can't see Matron Carpenter letting
a family with insufficient funds take one of her
children!" Lily and Sandy laughed and agreed.
Soon the three girls reached the Webbers' house.
Sandy parked her car and the three stepped out. The
Webbers' home was attractively landscaped and fairly
large. "What a marvelous place to raise children!"
Lily said. The other two girls agreed. After looking
around for a few more moments, the three walked up
to the house, following the path of stepping stones
laid around the flower beds. Sandy rang the doorbell
and soon a late middle-aged woman, smartly dressed
and wearing a tidy apron, opened the door.

"Mrs. Webber?" Sandy asked, holding out her
hand. "My name is Sandy Connors. I'm working with

the Santa Maria Police Department on the kidnapping
case of Lisa. This is Rose and her sister Lily. May
we come in?" The girls shook hands with the older
woman, who introduced herself as Maria Webber.
"Please, do come in," she said, holding the door
open. The three girls followed the woman inside and
saw the Webbers' house was tidy and clean. Sandy
admired a tastefully framed painting on the wall
behind the sofa. "That's a Monet, isn't it?"

"It's a print," Mrs. Webber said, "but yes, the
original painting was done by Monet. Henry, my
husband, got that for me on our twenty-fifth wedding
anniversary." She asked if she could get the three girls
anything to drink; all three politely declined. Soon the
group was seated in the living room. Sandy began by
asking Mrs. Webber, "How many children have you
fostered for the Home, Mrs. Webber?"

"Oh, I don't know. We have records of all of
them, but I can't remember off the top of my head. A
dozen, at least. Henry and I have no children of our
own and decided to raise foster children instead."
Sandy nodded, and asked how Lisa had been as
a foster child. "Oh she was an absolute dear! She
was the youngest child we had ever fostered, and I
was worried at first that there would be difficulties,
but she was such a dear, sweet baby. Of course she
cried at night sometimes and made a mess of herself
whenever she ate, but all babies do. We worked
with a lovely woman from the Home for the first few
weeks we had Lisa - she talked to us about how often
babies wake at night and how to tell if Lisa was crying
because she was hungry or wanted to be picked up or
if she wasn't feeling well - and she said that Lisa was
much quieter than most babies of that age. Of course,

I haven't worked with any children that young before, but Lisa was rarely any trouble. I don't work so I was able to take care of her all the time and only a few days were very challenging, and then I could always ask Henry for help when he got home from work. He's very good with children, you see, and he could always get little Lisa to stop crying." Mrs. Webber's eyes teared up as the told the girls about the child.

"Perhaps you three think I'm a foolish old woman for getting so upset about a foster child being taken, but Lisa was very dear to me and it quite broke my heart when she was kidnapped. Henry and I were actually talking about adopting her ourselves - we had become that attached to her. I don't know why she was so special to us; all the other children we've fostered were wonderful too and I grew fond of them as well, but Lisa is the first one we've honestly thought about adopting ourselves. She somehow seemed like our own child." Here the woman dabbed at her eyes with a delicate handkerchief. "Henry was also quite heartbroken when he found out Lisa had been taken. We immediately called the police, of course, and they came quickly and spoke with us."

"I understand you thought Betty Mullens might be a suspect?" Sandy asked. "Why is that?"

"Betty Mullens worked for me, helping me clean the house," Mrs. Webber explained. "She was very good at her job but was easily distracted by Lisa. I didn't think anything of it; Lisa was a very beautiful and happy child, I thought it natural that a woman would be distracted by her. Then the police asked if I knew anyone who showed an untoward interest in Lisa, and I felt I had to mention Betty. Her job was simple cleaning, nothing to do with the baby care

beyond occasionally laundering some of Lisa's things.
I noticed that she would do her work in a way that
would allow her to be in the same room as Lisa the
most often and would frequently go and peek in on
her between jobs. Like I said, I wasn't bothered by it.
Betty did all her work well and on time and she never
made a move to touch or pick up Lisa without asking.
She spoke to her in baby talk sometimes, but it truly
seemed completely innocent. I mentioned her to the
police, as she was one of the only people around Lisa,
besides Henry and me. Then when she didn't show
up for work the day after Lisa was taken the police
said she was a suspect. I tell you, I did not think Betty
Mullens was a kidnapper!"

"How did Betty Mullens come to be in your
employ, Mrs. Webber?" Sandy asked.

"Well, that's a funny thing, actually." Mrs. Webber
began, "We had had Lisa about three weeks. Henry
and I haven't employed a housekeeper before, but
I was finding that the extra chores required by such
a young child were beginning to wear on me. I
have had occasional trouble with my back, and the
cleaning and washing and broken sleep were causing
it to become painful. We thought we might have to
return Lisa to the Home, but even by then we were
attached to her and didn't want to do that. Henry had
the idea of hiring a woman to do some of the cleaning
tasks around the house so I would be free to spend
my time with Lisa and take care of her, and could
also rest a little during the day so that being woken in
the middle of the night wouldn't be such a problem.
I liked that plan, and thought I would begin to phone
employment agencies the next day to ask about a
temporary housekeeper. Well, right after breakfast the

next day, the doorbell rings and Betty Mullens is on the doorstep asking if I might want some help with house cleaning! She said she was going round the whole neighborhood asking. I thought it was a mite strange that she would be going door to door to find employment, but she provided good references and showed herself capable of doing the work so I hired her to come for a few hours each day. She only came while I was home and worked doing fairly simple tasks."

Sandy was sure this was an important clue. "Do you remember when Betty Mullens came to your door?" she asked. Mrs. Webber thought for a moment. "I believe it was a few weeks after we took Lisa home. It couldn't have been more than a month. I can get my records and see when I first paid her if you would like." Sandy said it would be useful to know and Mrs. Webber left the room.

CHAPTER 8

Less than a month! Sandy exchanged glances with Rose and Lily. "I'm sure that timing can't be a coincidence!" she said. Rose and Lily agreed it was very curious. "But Sandy, how would Betty Mullens have known that Mrs. Webber was looking for household help at that moment?" Rose asked. Sandy said she wasn't sure, but hoped that a few more questions would provide some answers. Soon Mrs. Webber returned, carrying a file. "I've checked in here," she said, "and I first paid Betty Mullens exactly five weeks after we brought Lisa home. I paid her every two weeks, so that would mean she began working here after we'd had Lisa for three weeks."

"Thank you, Mrs. Webber for being so cooperative with us. I have just a few more questions. When you and your husband spoke about getting some help around the house, were you at home?" Mrs. Webber looked surprised by the question. "We weren't, in fact. I don't know why I remember it so well, but I'm sure we were at our favorite Italian restaurant, the little one with the green awnings downtown. Why ever do you suppose that matters, my dear?"

"I'm not entirely sure," Sandy said. "I think perhaps Betty Mullens heard you mention you wanted some help and that's why she came the next day. I intend to speak to your neighbors and see if she really did go house to house, or if that was just a cover story." Mrs. Webber looked upset. "Do you mean to suggest that my husband and I were being spied on?"

"Oh no, nothing like that!" Sandy said lightly. "It's much more likely that Mrs. Mullens was needing a job and just overheard you. Many restaurants seat people quite close together and often you can't help but hear the conversation at the table next to you!" Mrs. Webber looked relieved. Sandy said she had only a few more questions. "Do you happen to remember the names of the references Betty Mullens provided?"

"No, dear, I'm sorry but I don't. She gave two, and I called them both. One was a hotel and the other was a private home. The men who answered gave very complimentary reviews of her work, and emphasized her work ethic. This proved to be true so I thought nothing else of it!" Sandy asked the woman if she had contact information for Betty. Mrs. Webber looked thoughtful. "I never did get any. She said she lived across town but never mentioned a street. She didn't give a phone number either. I suppose I was foolish not to ask, but my husband has always handled the business aspects of our life and it honestly did not occur to me that I would need a way to contact her! We set up a schedule and she said she would take her checks every other week. There was never any issue; she was on time to work every day and did her job quite well. The police asked if I had a phone number for her and that was the first moment that it occurred to me that it was strange she hadn't provided one."

Sandy thanked Mrs. Webber for her help and promised that if she found Lisa or Betty Mullens she would phone her. The three girls left Mrs. Webber's house and Sandy suggested they split up to ask the neighbors about any women that had approached them about working as a housekeeper. "We can each check three or four houses," Sandy said. "That way we won't miss anybody." Lily and Rose agreed and soon the three had spread out down the street. Sandy rang the doorbell of the house across the street from the Webbers first. And elderly woman answered. Sandy quickly introduced herself and said she was trying to track down a woman who might have worked as a housekeeper on this street. "Did anyone come to your house and offer to work for you within the past six months?" Sandy deliberately left the details vague to the woman wouldn't become alarmed.

"No, dear," the woman, who introduced herself as Madeline Carter, said. "No one has ever come to my door offering to clean my house. If I wanted a housekeeper, I would call the temp agencies. I don't know why a body would bother going door to door instead of just registering with one of them!" Sandy merely smiled and thanked the woman for her help. She went to the house next door but no one answered her ring. She spoke to people at the two houses further down the road but heard the same answer. "No one's stopped by looking for work here, I'm afraid!" she was told. At the final house, no one answered her ring. Sandy returned to her car and found Rose already there. "Any luck?" she asked.

"None." Rose said. "Not one of the people I spoke to remembered a woman coming by looking for cleaning work. At one of the houses there was nobody home." Sandy reported that she had gotten all the same answers, too. "It looks like Betty Mullens did not go door to door, but only went to the Webbers' house," Sandy said. "We'll see what Lily found out, but I would guess she'll have heard all noes, too." Soon Lily returned and confirmed Sandy's guess.

"Everyone I spoke to said no," Lily said, shaking her head. The three girls looked at each other. It seemed that Betty Mullens had not wanted a house-cleaning job, but rather had wanted a job at the Webbers' house!

"What do we do now, Sandy?" Rose asked. "We know more about what Betty Mullens did, but still don't know why she did any of it, or where she is now!" Sandy agreed there were still several key facts the girls were missing. Glancing at her watch, she noted that it was lunchtime. "How about we go to the Webbers' favorite Italian restaurant downtown. It's a long shot that any of the waiters will remember Betty Mullens, but I'd still like to ask." Rose and Lily agreed, though both thought it would be hopeless. "The Webbers probably went to that restaurant at least once a week!" Lily said. "Unless the Mullens were regulars, too, I doubt any of the wait staff will remember the specific night we're talking about."

"I agree, we're unlikely to get any new information, but at least we'll get a good meal!" Sandy smiled and soon the three were seated at a table near the window of the quaint restaurant. "Did you really mean that about Betty Mullens overhearing Mrs. Webber by chance, Sandy?" Rose asked as the girls looked over the menu. Sandy shook her head. "I didn't want to alarm her, but I'm fairly certain that the Mullens did not overhear that piece of information by accident. I still don't know why, but I feel that the Mullens, or Betty Mullens at least, has been interested in Lisa her whole life." Rose and Lily glanced at each other, uncertain where this hunch had come from. Sandy went on to explain that she felt sure Lisa hadn't randomly been picked for the kidnapping, but that there was a unifying thread to the whole case. "I don't know what it is yet, but once we find that, hopefully everything else will make more sense!"

At that moment a waiter came by and took the girls' orders. Sandy asked him nonchalantly if he knew the Webbers. "Oh yeah," the waiter said. "They come in often. I heard about their little girl getting kidnapped. That's a terrible thing." He shook his head. Sandy asked if they had ever been in and had any problems with other customers watching them or being too interested. The waiter looked puzzled, but said he couldn't remember anything. "Mrs. Webber, she gets upset easily I hear, so I think if she'd ever felt unsafe here she wouldn't have come back."

"Where did you hear that Mrs. Webber get upset easily?" Lily asked.

"Stevie mentioned it. He's worked here forever. We were talking about their little girl being taken and he said she must be a wreck, since she gets upset so easily. I guess one time they came in after there had been a small accident on their street and she was falling apart." Sandy thanked the man for the information and he went back to the kitchen. She sighed in frustration. "I know it was a slim chance, but I'd hoped to pick up a clue here," she confided to Rose and Lily. Lily patted Sandy's arm. "You can't expect to get clues everywhere," she said. "The food here looks good, so that makes the stop worthwhile." Sandy thanked her and agreed. Lily proved to be correct; the food was brought to the table quickly and was delicious.

The three girls enjoyed the meal and discussed their next move. Sandy said she wanted to find the car dealership where the Mullens had purchased their station wagon. "There are two dealerships in Santa Maria. If you two have time, I'd like to go there after lunch. If we can find the salesman who sold the

Mullens their vehicle, he may remember something about them." Rose said she thought this was also a bit of a stretch, but said she was willing to go with Sandy to question them. Lily agreed. The three girls finished their meal, paid, and soon were on the way to the car lots just outside of town.

CHAPTER 9

During the twenty minute drive to the car lots, the three girls discussed the mystery. Rose was particularly interested in the missing information. "Perhaps Betty Mullens heard that the Webbers were considering adopting Lisa and kidnapped her to hold her for ransom!" Sandy agreed this could be possible. "I think ransom demands are generally put in soon after the kidnappings occur. The Webbers haven't received any such demands." Lily jumped in, saying with an impish grin, "Maybe 'baby' Lisa isn't actually a baby! Maybe she's an older child with a rare disease and was kidnapped to avoid publicity about her illness!"

Rose and Sandy both laughed at that. "Maybe, she doesn't even really exist!" Rose said, determined to come up with the most ridiculous theory. "Maybe everyone is in cahoots and the whole kidnapping part is a fabrication to get Betty Mullens in trouble!" The three girls laughed again. As Sandy pulled her car into the lot, she said, "While we're thinking outside the box, I think we should acknowledge the possibility that baby Lisa could be an alien who wasn't kidnapped but merely returned to her home planet!" All three girls laughed. "Okay, Sandy," Rose said, "You win the crazy theories contest. Let's hope the car salesman has some more useful information!" Still giggling, the three stepped out of the car and walked over to the sales lot office.

Sandy introduced herself and the Pinkerton sisters to the young woman seated behind the counter. "I'm hoping to find some information about a couple that might have purchased a vehicle here, about eighteen months ago. The purchase was made by Peter and Betty Mullens." The young woman pulled a large binder off a shelf behind her and flipped through. "A couple by that name did purchase a white station wagon here August before last." Sandy counted up in her head; that was nineteen months ago. "I'm sure that's right," she said. "Is there any way that we could speak with the salesman who was in charge of the purchase?" The woman consulted the paper again. "You three are in luck; it was Mr. Levine who was in charge of that transaction. He's now the assistant manager. He should be in his office. Let me check and see if he's free." The secretary went to speak with him. Sandy smiled at the good luck.

"I was worried that the salesman might have moved on to another job," Sandy confided to Rose and Lily. "I'm glad to hear he's still working here."

"Miss Connors?" The secretary returned. "Mr. Levine can speak to you now." She showed the three into a side office. Sandy again introduced herself and her friends and reiterated her question. Mr. Levine thought for a few moments. "I do remember the Mullens, actually," he said. "I remember them because there was some difficulty finding anything to put as collateral for a loan. Mr. Mullens - his name began with a P; Paul, Peter, Parker, something like that ..."

"Peter Mullens," Sandy interjected.

"Yes, that was it," Mr. Levine continued. "He said that he and his wife were recently married and had just moved into town. They did not own a house in Santa Maria yet and had sold their last car before they moved. I talked about selling them an older model

that would require less money but they were insistent
on the new station wagon. When I couldn't give
them a loan, Mr. Mullens asked that I hold the car
for a week. I agreed, and a week later he came back
with the whole payment in cash! He said he had just
cashed the check that the buyer used to purchase his
previous car! He had a whole suitcase full of cash! It
did seem a little suspicious, but the firm's accountant
looked over the cash and said it was legal tender. He
put that down as a full payment and drove the car off
the lot - no loan or anything! It was a strange way to
do business, but I was assured it was legal and we
never ran into any trouble over it. I haven't seen the
Mullens since."

Sandy was intrigued by the story. "Did either of
the Mullens mention anything about where they were
from? Or where they were living in Santa Maria?"

"No. In fact, they didn't talk about themselves
much at all. I believe Mr. Mullens only mentioned
the recent move when the issue with securing the
loan came up. In fact, I asked where they had moved
from, just to make friendly conversation, and neither
one answered. I thought they were just upset about
the loan issues and maybe didn't hear. In retrospect,
I suppose it was a little odd. Can I ask why you're
asking about the Mullens?"

"I'm trying to find them," Sandy said simply. "Their
car was abandoned by my house and I'm looking for
them to return it." Sandy decided to say nothing about
the kidnapping case or her suspicions about Betty
Mullens' mental state. "Is that all you remember about
them?" Mr. Levine thought for a few moments. "That
is all I can remember now. If I recall anything else,
I'll be in touch." Sandy thanked the man for his time

and said she would leave contact information with the secretary. Soon the three girls were in the car and pulling out of the parking lot.

"That's interesting," Sandy said. "I wonder if the Mullens were deliberately being secretive or if they genuinely didn't hear Mr. Levine's questions."

"I think they were hiding something." Lily said flatly. "If I had just moved somewhere I would want to strike up conversations with people in my new town." Sandy agreed that it did seem odd. She reiterated that there was still a key piece of information that she was sure the girls were missing. "I'm most interested in the suitcase full of money that he mentioned. Perhaps he did cash a check at the bank, but maybe the money came from somewhere else."

"Sandy, are you suggesting that the Mullens were or are bank robbers?" Rose said. "I thought we were done coming up with ridiculous theories!"

"I realize it does sound unbelievable," Sandy said, smiling. "But it could be true. Think about it - two people show up in town, there are no records of them anywhere prior to this car registration. Peter Mullens claimed to have registered a car before but that didn't turn up in the police search, which indicates he may have changed his name before moving here. Then he buys a car with a suitcase full of cash. You have to admit it's not the most common story."

"Wouldn't there be a public record of the name change, though?" Rose asked.

"There would be, if they had gone through the proper legal channels," Sandy explained. "But, if they didn't change it legally or adopted it as an alias there would be no record. If the Mullens are criminals, or were, they would surely know someone from whom they could get false IDs for their new, adopted names." Rose and Lily agreed that it was a reasonable theory.

"It's at least possible," Lily said. "But then how does baby Lisa fit in? Why kidnap a child if they're trying to run away from their criminal past?" Sandy admitted she did not understand that piece yet. "I have a possible theory, but it may be way out there!" Rose and Lily asked what Sandy was thinking, but the young sleuth refused to share her theory. "Until I have some evidence to support it, I don't want to share it in case I'm completely wrong! I don't want you two to think I'm too crazy!"

"Sandy, we know you're crazy!" Lily laughed. "Why else would you take on a case like this?" Rose agreed, but assured the girl that she and her sister were just as crazy. "If you don't want to share your theory yet, that's just fine," the younger girl said. "But I hope some day you will tell us what it is, after you get some evidence to support it, that is!" All three girls laughed and continued to joke as Sandy drove back to the Pinkerton's house.

As Sandy approached the sisters' house, she reminded them that they were going to the downtown department stores tomorrow to speak to sales clerks. "If you do find one who sold baby clothes to Betty Mullens, I'd like to know when the sales occurred and also what the clerk's impression of Mrs. Mullens was - did she seem put together, or did she seem a little off?" The sisters promised to do what they could and said they would phone Sandy the next evening. Sandy dropped the girls off and then drove to her own house. She and her father ate dinner and watched a movie together before Sandy went to bed.

CHAPTER 10

The next morning Sandy awoke early. She went downstairs and ate breakfast with her father before he left for work. While the two were eating, she shared what she had learned the day before from the car salesman. "Dad, is there any way to check and see if the Mullens legally changed their name?" Sandy asked.

"I think the police might have ways to check; of course sometimes name changes are done for specific reasons and kept quiet," Mr. Connors reminded his daughter.

"You mean people in the witness protection program and similar things?" Sandy asked. Then she continued before her father had a chance to answer, "Dad, that would shed entirely new light on the case! If the Mullens were in hiding for their own safety before, they could be in serious trouble right now! Baby Lisa could be, too!" Mr. Connors reminded Sandy not to jump to conclusions.

"The police have ways of contacting the Federal Marshals and others who work to protect people in these kinds of programs," Mr. Connors added. "I'm sure that any calls that need to be made have been made." Sandy said she was still going to phone the police after breakfast to check on that angle. "I also want to hear about the progress on tracing Peter Mullens. I've been focused on recreating the Mullens past. I think the police were focusing on trying to find them and Lisa. I hope I haven't made a mistake in not focusing my energy on looking for all three."

"I feel that discovering a rational motive for the kidnapping is a very important step, dear," Mr. Connors said. "In no way do I think you've been wasting your time. You've found some very important things!" Sandy agreed, but said she still felt frustrated that a critical piece of information was eluding her. "I have faith that you'll find it soon enough," Mr. Connors said, patting his daughter's hand. "Why don't you discuss the mystery with your mother today when you pick her up? Perhaps a fresh viewpoint will tell you what you need to know!"

"That's a good idea, Dad. I'll do that." Sandy thanked him for his advice. Soon they finished breakfast and Mr. Connors left for work. Sandy, seeing that she didn't have to leave for the airport for another hour, phoned the police. Soon she was speaking to Officer Murray with whom she shared her thoughts about the Mullens being under some sort of protection. "We looked into that," the officer said, "when the case first came to light. We aren't privy to any details, of course, but we were able to find out that a couple by the name of Mullens is not under any sort of government protection by any agency, nor are there any couples that match the description of Peter and Betty missing from any agency. So I'm confident that we can cross that possibility off our list.

"We took your advice to check out Peter Mullens as well, and he has no records of any kind, aside from the car registration. The address they listed on the registration is abandoned. An old gentleman who is in a nursing facility down south owns it. The officer who spoke to him says he's quite senile but we're certain he was not renting the house to the Mullens. There is no other record of a domicile for the couple, nor are there birth certificates, insurance records or anything else."

"So Mullens must be an adopted name," Sandy said. "Has anyone recorded a legal name change to Mullens recently?"

"Fourteen people in the last two years, according to US government records," Officer Murray said. "We've checked on them- twelve are women who were married to men named Mullens- none of the men named Peter, and none of the women named Betty- and the other two were children- both under the age of ten- who took the last name Mullens after being adopted. We're waiting for a list from the registry office of all the people legally named Mullens in this country as of now, but I feel certain that we won't find the Mullens for whom we're searching."

"This is frustrating," Sandy sighed. "It's almost like they don't exist! Except we know they do because they kidnapped a child!" Officer Murray agreed that it was proving to be a challenge. "We've alerted all of our street officers to keep their eyes open and have conducted several traffic stops but no one matching the descriptions of Peter or Betty Mullens has been found. We're going to continue searching; if you find anything about their previous locations or any sort of motive please let us know." Sandy assured the officer she would and said goodbye. She still had some time before she needed to leave so she sat down with a book and read for a while. "Maybe reading this book about art will clear my brain enough for me to figure out what we're missing!" Though the young sleuth read for almost half an hour, no new ideas occurred to her. "Oh well," she mused. "Maybe Mother will have a new idea about the case."

Sandy got in her car and drove to the nearby airport. After parking and walking in, she stepped up to the ticket counter to inquire about the flight from Phoenix. She was pointed to a gate near the end of the terminal and walked down there. Noticing that there were still fifteen minutes until the flight was scheduled to land, Sandy thought perhaps she could ask the airport personnel if they had seen anyone resembling the Mullens flying out in the past week. "Maybe they escaped using another assumed name!" she thought. She put the question to several airline workers and baggage handlers, asking if a couple matching that description had been seen with a child, but no one remembered seeing them. One of the baggage handlers declared that he had not seen a six-month-old child in the airport at all in the last week. "If you're looking for a kid, ma'am," he said, "that babe didn't fly from here. At least not during my shift."

"Thank you," Sandy said, looking at her watch and noting that it was the scheduled time for her mother's plane to arrive. She walked back to the assigned gate and was just in time to see the aircraft pull up. Sandy waited eagerly until she saw her mother deplane and walk to the terminal doorway. She rushed up to greet her and the two hugged. Then, taking her mother's carry-on, they went to baggage claim. Fortunately, Mrs. Connors' bag was among the first to reach the carousel and the two were soon back in Sandy's car leaving the airport. Mrs. Connors told about her visit to her sister, saying that the city of Phoenix was beautiful, and sunny and warm. Thinking about the time change, Sandy suggested that the two stop for an early lunch at a restaurant near the highway. Mrs. Connors agreed, saying she was fairly hungry, and soon the two were seated.

After they ordered their food, Sandy told her mother about the case. She shared her worries that there was some crucial fact that was eluding her. Mrs. Connors listened intently. By the time Sandy told the whole story, their food had arrived and the two began to eat. After a few bites, Mrs. Connors said, "Sandy, I don't know much about what would compel a woman to change her name and move somewhere far away, mysteriously, as these Mullens surely did, but I think I know why she kidnapped the baby." Sandy listened intently.

"As the police said, ransom notes are usually delivered shorty after the kidnapping occurs. Since it has been almost a week and there's no note yet, I think we can safely assume this isn't a kidnapping for ransom." Sandy agreed, and asked her mother to continue. "So, the question becomes why was baby Lisa kidnapped? Now, I can't say for sure," Mrs. Connors said, "But I can take a guess as a woman and a mother and I think that, without the appearance of a ransom note, you have to think Mrs. Mullens kidnapped the child to keep her safe! I can't imagine why else a woman would kidnap a child and not submit a ransom note."

Sandy was surprised. "That's a possibility we hadn't thought of," she said. "I am a little concerned about the possibility that Mrs. Mullens may be mentally unstable and thus there may not be a logical reason."

"That could be," Mrs. Connors conceded. "But when you spoke to Mrs. Webber did she mention anything that led you to believe her former employee was mentally ill?"

"No, actually just the opposite," Sandy admitted. "Mrs. Webber said that Betty Mullens was quite capable, learned her job quickly and did it well."

"In that case, I think you should consider the possibility that Betty Mullens kidnapped Lisa to keep her safe from something. And if that's the case, the question you need to answer next is, from what does Lisa need to be kept safe?"

CHAPTER 11

Sandy was surprised by the logic of her mother's theory. "I can't believe I didn't think of that!" she chided herself.

"Now, dear," her mother said, "don't be upset with yourself for not thinking of it first. I'm the only person with children that you've spoken to about this, so my perspective is naturally different. Barring the possibility that Betty Mullens is unstable, which I think is unlikely given her work record, the only reason I can think of for a stable, upright woman to take a child is to protect it."

"That does make sense," Sandy said. "It fits with something that I've been thinking, though I have no clues to support it, and that's that Betty Mullens may be baby Lisa's mother!"

"Hmmm ..." Mrs. Connors thought for a few moments. "That would make even more sense, actually. Why would a woman unrelated to a child go to such lengths to protect her as to commit a crime? Of course, if that is the case, then the legal part gets complicated, doesn't it? Depending on how Lisa came to be separated from her mother it may not be kidnapping!"

"Lisa was surrendered at the Santa Maria General Hospital, so the mother forfeited all right," Sandy reminded her mother.

"Yes, well, that's assuming that it was her mother that surrendered her!" Mrs. Connors said.

"Oh my!" Sandy was shocked. "We could be investigating the wrong case! What if Lisa was kidnapped before she was surrendered and Betty

Mullens didn't commit a crime, but rather righted the original kidnapping case? Of course, she should have reported the kidnapping six months ago."

"Perhaps she was afraid to, for some reason," Mrs. Connors said. "There's still the very suspicious, in my opinion, matter of the sneaky name change. And we know nothing about the Mullens' history!" Sandy agreed that this was true. She sighed. "There's still so much we don't know!" Her mother agreed that the case was quite convoluted at this point. "I am sure you'll find the answers soon, though!" She said. "Didn't Rose and Lily agree to do some sleuthing for you today?"

"Yes, they did," Sandy said. "Perhaps they have found something that will provides a clue. I must call the Pinkerton house as soon as we get home!" The two spent the rest of the lunch hour discussing the mystery but were unable to come up with any new answers. Soon they finished and after paying the bill returned to the car. The rest of the drive went quickly and it was just past 3 o'clock when they returned home. Sandy helped carry her mother's bags into the house, and then went to use the telephone. She was quickly connected to the Pinkerton household; Rose and Lily's mother answered the phone.

"Hello, Mrs. Pinkerton, it's Sandy Connors," Sandy said. "Are Rose and Lily home?" Mrs. Pinkerton said that her daughters were still out. "They said they were going on a sleuthing expedition!" she laughed, "you must have taught them well!" Sandy explained that she had asked the girls to do some sleuthing for her while she was picking her mother up from the airport. She asked Mrs. Pinkerton to please have her daughters return the phone call when they got home.

Mrs. Pinkerton assured Sandy she would pass along
the message. After chatting for a few more moments,
Sandy bid the woman goodbye.

"Maybe that means Rose and Lily are picking up
some great clues!" Sandy said. She went upstairs to
help her mother unpack and shared her hopes. Mrs.
Connors laughed. "You've certainly turned those two
into good detectives!" Sandy laughed and agreed.
The two quickly unpacked Mrs. Connors' suitcase
and soon moved downstairs. After debating for a few
moments what to do while awaiting a return call,
Sandy decided to bake cookies to bring to the Wrights
and their visiting family. "After all," she said, "it's really
because of them that I found this mystery, so I should
say thank you!" Again her mother laughed and said
she was sure the family would appreciate the treat.

Sandy found her favorite recipe and had just
put the first sheet of cookies into the oven when
the phone rang. Her mother answered it, but soon
gestured to Sandy, saying it was Lily Pinkerton.
Excited, Sandy hurried to the phone. "Hi! What's the
news?" she asked. Lily said she and Rose had made
some interesting discoveries. "Can we come over
now and talk to you? We've just gotten home from
our expedition and are bursting to tell!" Sandy said
that would be fine. Lily said she and Rose would be
over in five minutes. Sandy washed the baking dishes
while she waited, and soon the doorbell rang.

She let the two girls in and they sat in the living
room. "So," Sandy began, "what's all this great news?"
Rose and Lily looked at each other then finally Rose
said, "We think Betty Mullens and Lisa are still in
Santa Maria!" Sandy gasped, and asked the two to
explain.

"We did what you asked," Lily began. "We went to the downtown department stores and asked at the children's department in each store about a woman matching her description. In both department stores" - Sandy recalled that there were two main department stores in Santa Maria, Brooke and Sons and the smaller Michael's - "we found a clerk who remembered her! Betty went to both stores on the same day, the day before Lisa disappeared. She bought clothes, a few toys, a diaper bag, blankets and bottles. The department store doesn't sell formula but she almost certainly purchased that in a grocery store. In Michael's we spoke to the clerk who sold her the things, and she said that the same woman had come back that very morning to get some new blankets and bibs! Both times and in both stores she paid with cash, but the clothes she bought and the woman match the descriptions!"

Sandy was shocked. "I was sure they had left town; why would they stay here when she's wanted for kidnapping? And where are they hiding? How is she getting around since she abandoned her car?" Rose said she didn't know.

"None of the clerks saw the woman arrive or leave so we don't know if she walked or drove. She didn't have a child with her when she was shopping this morning, either."

"That seems to confirm that Peter Mullens, or at least someone else, is with her and must have been keeping Baby Lisa safe." Sandy commended the sisters on the good work. "Now we have something definite to begin work on- tracing Betty Mullens in Santa Maria!" Sandy shared her mother's idea about the reason for the kidnapping with the Pinkertons.

Lily said it made sense; "Why else would someone be purchasing nice, new clothes for a child? Certainly she isn't holding her for ransom, so she clearly intends to take good care of her." Rose agreed it was the most logical idea.

"Do you think that Lisa was kidnapped from Betty Mullens six months ago, before she was surrendered?" Rose asked.

"I'm not sure," Sandy said. "If that is the case, then we have an unknown kidnapper to find, and we should work on exonerating Betty Mullens! She may be wanted by the police for kidnapping her own child!" Rose and Lily agreed that they should do what they can to clear her name, if she is in fact innocent. Lily voiced her concerns, saying, "If she's innocent, why are there no records of her? And why didn't she report the kidnapping six months ago?" Sandy agreed that it was still suspicious.

"Whichever theory turns out to be correct, we still have a lot of sleuthing to do." At that moment, the timer rang and Sandy excused herself, saying she had a batch of cookies in the oven. While Sandy was in the kitchen the doorbell rang and Lily said she would answer it since Sandy's hands were full. Sandy heard Lily go to the door and then gasp. She quickly put down the cookie sheet and went to see what was the matter. Sandy gasped too.

Betty Mullens and the kidnapped child, Lisa, were standing on her front step!

CHAPTER 12

Sandy stepped back in surprise. Betty Mullens looked nervous; she held the sleeping child against her body so that the baby's face was hidden and glanced around several times before speaking. "Please let me come inside," she said. "I know this is a terrible imposition on you but please let me explain what's happened!" Seeing the woman's distress, Sandy motioned for her to step inside and closed the door. Betty was immediately relieved. "I don't believe I was followed here, but I must be so careful now. Thank you for letting me explain." Sandy showed Betty to the living room. Rose looked up in surprise but Sandy merely said, "This is Betty Mullens. She's come to tell us what has happened to her."

Betty sat down on a chair near the fireplace. She glanced around the room and said hesitantly, "I don't want to be rude, but is there any way we could close these curtains? I'm so worried about - well, I'll tell you the whole story in just a minute but right now I'd like to make sure I'm safe here for a half hour at least." Sandy assured the woman she would be safe in the Connors' house and quickly pulled all the curtains closed. She turned on the table lamps and lit a fire, which gave the room a cheery glow and cozy warmth. "Please, Mrs. Mullens, tell us your story," Sandy asked as she sat back down.

"It's been such a confusing time…which parts do you want to hear?"

"Please tell the whole thing," Sandy requested, saying she had some ideas about certain things but would like to hear the entire story from beginning to end. Betty acquiesced, and began. "First, please call me Betty. Mrs. Mullens is far too formal. The story begins almost twenty years ago, when my husband, Peter, was young. I did not know him then. He lived in a large city back east - he's never told me which city for safety reasons. Peter wound up out on his own when he was a teenager. I don't know the details, but I'm sure it was a very hard time for him. He fell in with some people who were bank robbers. I guess having a small, young child can be useful in some of the jobs ... again I don't know details. I only know that by the time Peter was twenty he was a wanted criminal but also a very wealthy man.

"He decided at that point that he had had enough of that life and tried to leave. The gang he was with made it very hard for him to go, and he's described sneaking out of the city late at night and being on the run for several years. Fortunately for him, shortly after he ran, several of the bosses of the gang were arrested and that took the focus off his escape. He changed his name to Peter Carlson and went to Chicago. I met him there almost four years ago. I was working as a kindergarten teacher and he had a part time job helping the football coach at the high school in my district. Anyway, we were married three years ago. He told me about his past before we married, but I knew that all of that was truly over. My husband is a good man, you must know that. He was put in terrible circumstances when he was young and he found a way to make it work by turning to crime but he truly has given all of that up now."

"We all believe that, Betty," Sandy reassured the woman. Lily and Rose nodded in assent, and Betty continued. "We lived in Chicago happily for several

months until Peter became worried. He didn't tell
me details - he did everything he could to protect me
from that part of his past - but he said he thought he
was being watched and followed sometimes. So we
decided to change our names and move. We sold
our car to a shady dealer who would give us cash,
boarded a bus and left in the middle of the night. I
wanted to come to the coast and Peter said he knew
a man in Santa Maria who would help us out. I guess
the man was a friend who had also escaped from
the gang and created a new, quiet life for himself out
here. When we got here, his friend let us stay at his
house in exchange for cooking and cleaning - the
man was getting old - and he also got us new IDs with
our new name. And so we became Peter and Betty
Mullens.

"We bought a car and Peter began to volunteer
at several local children's organizations. He used
a different name for that, Booker." Sandy said that
explained why the police had not found a single trace
of him in any records, aside from the car registration.
"Yes, he wanted to be anonymous in his new town.
I think he was still worried that we would be found,
even here. Things went very well for several months,
and that was when I found out I was expecting a
child. Peter was ecstatic - he loves children, and so
do I. I thought we were safe here so I wasn't worried
about the child's safety. Peter had another ID made for
me that I used when I went to check ups, so the baby
was legally born to Peter and Betty Booker. This is
Lisa, my child." Rose and Lily gasped.

"Baby Lisa, the baby you're wanted for kidnapping,
is your daughter?" Rose asked. Betty nodded. "I'll
tell you how that came about in a moment. Shortly

before Lisa was born, Peter again became worried that we had been discovered. He thought we should run again, but I was going to give birth any day and I couldn't travel with a newborn. I was also loath to leave her behind. The only thing we could think to do was to surrender her to the Santa Maria hospital before the men chasing us found out who she was. I only agreed to do it because I wanted her safe." Betty wiped tears from her eyes and was quiet for several seconds. "Peter convinced me that the men who were chasing us would harm her if they found us so we crept to the back door late one night when she was only a week old and left her there. It was a terrible decision, but we had no choice. Peter didn't want to go to the police about the people chasing us because he was worried he would be arrested for the robberies.

"Peter thought we should leave town, but I refused to leave my child. I watched from a distance as she was sent to the Home for children, then as she was given to a foster family. I followed them around town several times to see if they were a nice family for my baby to live with. I happened to overhear at dinner one night that the woman, Maria Webber, was looking for some help around the house. Peter thought it was too dangerous but I was insistent; I had to be near my child! So the next day I went to the Webbers' house and offered my services as a housekeeper. I forged references and gave phone numbers that would all ring at our house where Peter's old friend told fake stories about how well I had worked at his hotel and as his housekeeper. The trick worked and Mrs. Webber hired me. I did good work for her, even though I didn't have to be working, but every chance I got I would sneak in to see my darling girl. The Webbers took good care of her.

"Peter and I were planning to adopt her once the danger had passed; we thought the man chasing us could be paid off or gotten rid of somehow. I didn't ask what Peter was planning because I really didn't want to know, I just wanted us to be safe but mostly I wanted Lisa safe. Sadly, before he could take care of things, the evil man found out where Lisa was. Peter got a threatening note one day that said the man knew where Lisa was and was going to kidnap her the next night. We decided to take her first and hide. So the next afternoon, before Mrs. Webber put Lisa down for her nap, I hid in the closet in my little girl's room. After Mrs. Webber left, I crept out, turned the baby monitor off and took Lisa. She was such a good girl and didn't cry at all. We crept out the back door and went to our house. Peter's old friend died a few months ago, so we had the whole house to ourselves. We hid there.

"I went out to buy baby stuff and groceries, but beyond that we haven't left the house. Until last night. Peter said he had seen a note for him in the classifieds the day before that indicated a meeting place and time and he was going to take care of it. He expected to be back within a few hours, but he didn't return. I'm terribly worried about him. I came to you to tell you my story because I knew you would listen. I know you'll have to turn me in to the police now but I feel that finding Peter is worth that. I hope that, after he's found, we can clear this matter up so he and I can legally adopt Lisa and we won't have to live in hiding anymore!"

CHAPTER 13

Sandy, Rose and Lily listened to the story, amazed. After Betty finished talking there was a moment of silence in the room. Finally Lily spoke up, "That's an incredible story! We've been thinking of the wrong person as the bad guy - here we thought you had kidnapped Lisa to ransom her or otherwise do her harm and you've been protecting her! What a mix up!" Rose chimed in also, apologizing for the confusion. "I hope we can help to solve this misunderstanding."

"Betty," Sandy said suddenly, "Was it the Santa Maria Chronicle in which your husband read this note?"

"Yes, it must have been. That's the only paper we get." Sandy smiled and stood up.

"I'm going to get our copy of yesterday's paper. Perhaps we can find the note and figure out where Peter went!" Sandy excused herself to look for the paper. Rose shook her head, "That's our Sandy; doesn't waste a single moment!" Betty laughed and said she was glad the three were willing to help. "I'm so pleased you three believe me! I would have come to ask for help sooner, but I was worried no one would listen!" Both Pinkerton sisters assured Betty that Sandy was always willing to help someone in need.

"Betty," Lily asked, "Just one thing I'm wondering, and that is how you knew to come to Sandy's house to tell your story. Did someone recommend you come here?"

"No," Betty shook her head. "I don't think I would have trusted anyone's recommendation! I read in the newspaper a few months back an article about the wonderful job Sandy did - with your help, I believe - solving that mystery about a stolen ring. I thought that if I were ever in trouble and couldn't go to the police that I would come here." Rose smiled. She said she remembered that article. "It left out most all of the good detective work and clues Sandy found, though!" She related how the young sleuth had even been kidnapped by the villain before finding the treasure. "It was really the kidnapping that led us to the treasure!" Lily interjected. "We found the stolen ring in the kidnapper's house where Sandy was held prisoner!"

At this moment Sandy reentered the room. She laughed to hear Rose and Lily telling the story of their previous success. Sandy was inclined to downplay her successes, saying that she had gotten very lucky and received some invaluable advice and help from friends and family. "It was really all the help that allowed me to solve the mystery!" she said, as she unfolded the classifieds section of the Santa Maria paper. "Fortunately, this section was small yesterday," she said, handing the first page to Betty. "Why don't you and Rose go over this page while Lily and I will look over the second page? If you see anything that looks suspicious, circle it. We'll all go over the possible messages after we're done and then, Betty, you can tell us which one seems the most logical."

Betty looked a little nervous at that, saying that she didn't know the code her husband and his former associates used. Sandy said to just look for any ad that didn't seem to match with the rest of the ads. She assured the woman that all three girls would talk over any ad she pointed out and that they would decide as a group. Looking slightly more confident, Betty set to work. Sandy and the Pinkerton sisters did likewise. For a few minutes the only sounds in the room were the rustlings of newsprint and the slight scratches of a pencil as the girls circled any ads that seemed to them unnatural. Before long the four had read over all the ads. Each had circled at least one.

Rose read out the one she circled first: "Son seeking remuneration from family for theft of oranges. Submit to bank for Son by weekend," she read. "That seems strange to me. Why would a son put an ad like that in the classifieds? Why not just call his family?" Sandy agreed that it was unusual, but she felt it had no meaning beyond the stated. "Listen to this one, though," she continued, reading slowly, "Redman must find himself. If you seek the truth you must look the devil in the eye. I'll be seeing you in all the old familiar places. Come only if you dare. That's a strange ad!" Rose and Lily agreed that it certainly was unusual. "Betty, does this mean anything to you?" Sandy asked.

"I think it does," she answered slowly. "I don't know many specifics about my husband's past, but I've heard him mumbling in his sleep about 'Redman' and a devil. I didn't ask about it at the time." Sandy was elated; she was sure this was the clue for which they were searching. She asked the others to read the ads they had circled, but none seemed to offer any clues. "I'm certain this ad is the one we're trying to find!" She declared. "Now, we must find out what it means!" She suggested that they brainstorm possible ideas and Betty could share whether they seemed plausible or not. The woman agreed, and soon Lily had an idea.

"Is it possible that this 'Redman' is one of the gang - perhaps the leader?" Betty said it was possible. Rose chimed in that 'Redman' could perhaps be gang alias for Peter himself. Sandy said she thought that sounded logical. "Then the devil mentioned would be the person Peter was meeting - perhaps a former boss or high level associate." Betty said that would make sense.

"Peter said that the gang used aliases for the members and that the bosses took grand names upon themselves. He didn't mention any at the time, but 'devil' would fit that pattern."

"Alright, so let's take that as a working hypothesis," Sandy said. "Then we're left with the last two lines. I'll be seeing you in all the old familiar places. Of course that's from a song, but I don't think that's what he means." Rose suggested that perhaps the clue meant they were meeting at a concert where that song would be featured. "Or maybe the 'devil' is a performer who sings that song!" Sandy said she felt this part of the clue was telling Peter where to meet the 'devil.'

"If the two were formerly familiar with each other and their habits, then saying this would indicate that he expects to meet in a place where they formerly spent a lot of time together," Sandy said.

"A bank!" Betty chimed in. "If that's the case, then it must be a bank. They were bank robbers and Peter said that they were careful never to be seen together anywhere. They met to plan the jobs in secret locations but apparently they never used a meeting place more than once. So the only place where they

were together more than one time would be the banks
they robbed!" All three agreed that was a reasonable
assumption. "That doesn't help narrow it down hardly
at all, though!" Lily complained. "There must be
dozens of different banks!"

"But only a few in Santa Maria. Betty, you say your
husband saw this ad in yesterday's paper and went
to meet the man last night. What time did he leave?"
Sandy asked.

"Around ten o'clock. He said he expected to be
back before midnight," Betty answered, beginning to
tear up. Rose put her arm around the woman.

"That would indicate that the meeting place was
in Santa Maria or very nearby. If he planned on the
meeting being half an hour, at least, that leaves forty-
five minutes to drive to and from the location," Sandy
concluded.

"Betty," Rose began suddenly, "how did Peter drive
to the meeting place? Your car is still in the police
garage!"

"Oh, Peter has been using his old friend's car, the
one who recently passed away. It's an old brown
sedan. It drives well but attracts no attention so he
said it was safer than our new station wagon. Plus
he was worried that the people chasing us knew the
license place number and could follow the car," Betty
explained.

"Well that makes it easier!" Sandy said, feeling
foolish not to have thought of that question herself.
"We can get a list of all the banks within forty-five
minutes drive of here, go to them and leave a request
for the night watchman to tell us if he saw any men
outside the bank last night around 11 PM, and if
so what kinds of vehicles they came in. We should

be able to find the right bank within a day!" Betty expressed gratitude for Sandy's help. Sandy glanced at her watch, and said she thought it was too late to do that this evening. "Betty, if it's okay with you, I think we should go to the police station and tell the story to the officers there. I'm sure they'll believe you, and they can keep you and your daughter protected and also begin to look for your husband." Reluctantly, Betty agreed and soon the two left for the station. Rose and Lily went home, after bidding them good night and promising to be at the Connors' house early the next morning to begin the hunt.

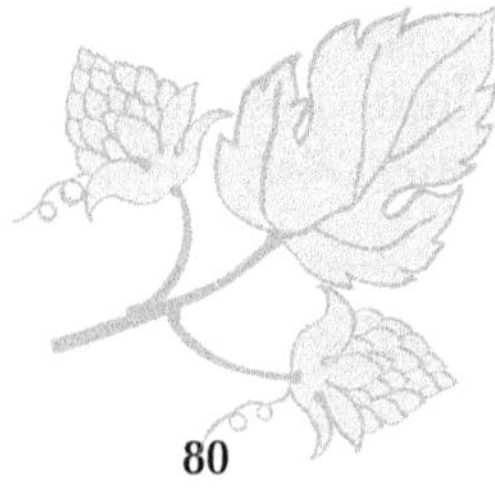

CHAPTER 14

Sandy drove Betty and baby Lisa to the police station. Betty was very quiet, looking out the window at the darkened streets. Sandy sensed that Betty was nervous about going to the police. "Betty, the authorities will help you. If you tell them the whole story about your husband and the threats; they'll keep you and your daughter safe."

"Peter always had a hard time trusting police. I guess because when he was young and needed help he didn't get any from them, and then he was wanted for crimes he committed only to keep himself alive. I know that my husband never stole for fun or for luxuries. Then as soon as he could, he got out, but he's never really learned to trust the police."

"Do you think he's worried that he could still be arrested for the robberies?" Sandy asked gently.

"I think he is. I think he's also worried about what will happen to me if the police find out that I've known where he was all these years and never turned him in." Sandy assured the woman that she would not be held responsible for her husband's former crimes. "The primary goal of the police in this case is to find your daughter, and to keep her safe. It's on that they will focus."

"But, Sandy, what if they don't believe me? I have Lisa's birth certificate here and an ID identifying me as Betty Booker, her mom, and the first threatening note. Will that be enough?" Sandy said she would go in with her and speak to the officers. "I know the two officers who have been assigned to this case; we'll show them all these papers and make them see that your story is true." Sandy reached the police station and parked her car. After a momentary hesitation, Betty got out of the vehicle, still carrying her young daughter. Sandy carried the bag of Lisa's things that Betty thought to bring and they walked toward the station. Sandy continued to offer encouraging words as they walked.

Once inside the station, Sandy asked to speak to either Officer Crowley or Officer Murray. The receptionist, who recognized Sandy, went to tell the officers she had arrived. Soon Officer Murray stepped into the waiting room. Sandy said that she had brought someone to speak to him confidentially and asked that the three be shown into a private room. The secretary directed them into a room down a hallway. She closed the door behind them. Betty looked around at the small, sparsely furnished room nervously, but Sandy smiled encouragingly and soon the three were seated.

"Officer Murray," Sandy began, "This is Betty Mullens. She came to my house to explain what happened. She's brought Lisa, her daughter, and is in need of protection. I will let her tell you her story." Officer Murray looked shocked. He turned to Betty, his mouth agape, and saw the sleeping child in her arms. "This is the kidnapped child we've been searching for? Lisa, who was being fostered by the Webbers?" Sandy nodded, saying only, "Lisa Mullens is her name."

"Do you mean to say that Lisa, the kidnapped child, is the daughter of the woman who kidnapped her?" The officer turned to look at Betty Mullens. "This is your daughter?" Betty nodded, holding Lisa close to her body. Officer Murray passed a hand over his face, momentarily lost for words. Sandy took the opportunity to speak. "Officer," she began, "I know this sounds incredible but please listen to Betty's story. She has papers and documents to prove her story is true." Officer Murray said he would certainly be interested to hear, so Betty told the entire story again. When she got to Lisa's birth, she showed the man the birth certificate and her alternate ID. "Officer, I know it's against the law to use false identification but do you see how we had no choice?" Officer Murray assured the woman that if her story proved to be true she would not be prosecuted about the use of false identification.

Betty continued telling her story, showing Officer Murray the threatening note she and Peter had received in the mail. Sandy interrupted her to ask how the note had gotten to her, "I thought your address was a secret?" Betty said that it was, and then explained. "Peter used to check the post office general delivery for letters to Peter and Betty Mullens, as well as a few of the names he'd used previously. One day this letter was left for us, addressed to the Mullens, general delivery. So that was how he knew that we'd been found out but that our house was still safe. I still have no idea how these people found out we were in Santa Maria, and using the name Mullens." Betty looked very upset and Sandy put her arm around the woman's shoulder. Officer Murray said that criminals had access to large webs of information, much of it gathered illegally. He then encouraged Betty to continue with her story. Gathering her courage, she finished by explaining why her husband left and the theory Sandy and the Pinkertons had proposed about where he went.

"That's a very logical theory," Officer Murray said. He assured Betty that he believed her story. "This evidence is compelling, and this story answers all the questions about the case. I will send out a bulletin to our patrol cars to speak to the night watchmen at the relevant banks; with any luck by morning we'll know which bank it is we're looking for," here the man hesitated for a few moments, then continued, "Mrs. Mullens, I know your story is correct and we won't be arresting you for kidnapping, but I'm afraid I must take you and your daughter into custody." Sandy and Betty both gasped, but Officer Murray held up his hand. "Let me explain why," he said. "First, until we can get a judge to rescind the warrant - which I will personally take care of first thing tomorrow morning, I'm legally bound to hold you. If I let you walk out that door then I will be breaking the law and I'll have to arrest myself and your warrant will still be outstanding and that just creates more mess. The second, and most compelling reason is that I believe you and your daughter are in danger. I know your house was a safe place up until last night, but these criminals are clearly very determined and if they traced you here it wouldn't be hard for them to find your house. Because that's the case, I think the only way to ensure your safety- and Lisa's safety - is to take the two of you into protective custody for the night. To be clear, I am not arresting you. I will take the two of you to a safe location where you will stay with one of our matrons for the night."

Betty looked upset, but said, "I suppose that's the only real option we have. I worry about what will happen if Peter returns home and finds me gone, though." Officer Murray said he would send a patrolman to watch the house. "If your husband returns home, he'll be informed that you're safe. We will have to take him into protective custody, as well," the officer said. Still looking upset, Betty agreed.

"I think we have no choice," she said grimly.

"Officer," Sandy said suddenly, "can Betty stay at my house for the night? I'm sure she'll be safe there." Officer Murray looked thoughtful. He said he was going to excuse himself to speak with his superiors about the situation. "I admit, I have little experience with our protective custody arrangements," he said. He then left the room, saying he would return in a few minutes. As soon as he had left Betty turned to Sandy and said gratefully, "Oh thank you! I never would have had the courage to come here without you!" Sandy smiled and said that she was glad for any help she could offer. "I hope you'll be allowed to stay with us. I'm sure that will make you feel more at home." Betty smiled and agreed.

At that moment Officer Murray returned, with a middle-aged woman walking behind him. "Betty, Sandy, this is Mrs. March. She is one of our matrons. If you want to stay at Sandy's house over the night, Mrs. Mullens, then the law requires a matron to stay as well. Mrs. March has volunteered. Sandy, will that work?" Sandy agreed to the arrangement immediately. Officer Murray said he would also station a policeman on Sandy's street for the night. "If anything happens, call the station. We'll have someone on the phones all night. I will also phone the Webbers in the morning to let them know that Lisa has been found, and is safe." Sandy and Betty thanked the officer, and then left with Mrs. March, and Sandy drove home. She was pleased with the arrangement and felt sure that Betty Mullens and baby Lisa would be safe at her home over the night.

Betty Mullens sat quietly in the car, and soon the three women were back at the Connors' house. Sandy was pleased to note that a police car was parked across the street. She pointed it out to Betty and again assured her she would be safe. Mrs. March commented that the Connors' house was an ideal location for keeping someone safe. "The winding driveway and large open garden will make it very hard for anyone to hide while approaching the house." Sandy chimed in that the family had lights by the front door and sides of the house. "I'll get Dad to leave them on tonight," Sandy said, smiling.

Inside, Sandy found her parents eating a late dinner. She hugged them both and introduced Betty Mullens and Mrs. March. Mr. Connors' eyebrows went up when he heard the name Mullens, but he merely asked the three women if they had already eaten. All said they had. Sandy, seeing that Betty Mullens looked tired and anxious about getting her child to bed, gave her father a brief summary of Betty's story and explained how the she and Mrs. March happened to be staying with them over the night. She assured him that the next day she would tell the full story. She then showed the women to the guest bedroom, saying she would make up a bed for Mrs. March on the sofa.

"Betty, is Lisa old enough to share the bed with you? If not, I think we still have an old crib in the attic I could get," Sandy offered. Betty assured her that Lisa would do well in the large guest bed. Betty carried Lisa's diaper bag into the nearby bathroom while

Sandy put sheets and blankets on the sofa for Mrs. March. Soon the two were ready for bed, and after Betty had finished settling Lisa down, Sandy said good night. She returned to the kitchen and sat down with her parents. "I should probably be going to bed," she said, commenting on the busy day she was certain she would have tomorrow, "but I'm too keyed up! This has been a breakthrough day on the case!" She again summarized the story for her parents, this time adding in more details.

"And here I thought we were looking for Betty and Peter Mullens to arrest them for kidnapping, when really they're the ones that need the help!" She shook her head in disbelief. Her father asked how Sandy and Mrs. Mullens had been able to prove her story to the police. Sandy explained about the birth certificate, threatening note and false ID Betty had shown. "I know it's against the law to use a false ID, but I think the police are going to dismiss that charge in Betty's case," Sandy said. "Tomorrow morning, Officer Murray is going to go to the judge's office to get the warrant for her arrest rescinded. Tonight, she's technically in police custody - primarily for her and her daughter's protection. That's why matron March is staying with us as well. She should be safe here." Sandy asked her father if it would be all right to leave the lights on all night. He assured her it was, and said he would double-check all the doors and windows before going to bed that night.

"Thanks, Dad," Sandy said. She kissed her parents good night and went up to her room. Though the young sleuth was still excited by the day's events, she fell asleep quickly and slept well. She awoke shortly after dawn and, unable to contain her curiosity,

pulled a robe on and crept down the hall to peek into
the guest room. She was relieved to see both Betty
and Lisa still sleeping soundly. Opening the door
another crack, she saw Mrs. March on the guest sofa.
Sandy heaved a sigh of relief and went downstairs to
prepare breakfast. She knew her father would come
down shortly to eat before he left for work, and heard
her parents moving about on the floor above. They
appeared shortly and the three ate breakfast together
before Mr. Connors left for work. Sandy and her
mother washed the dishes, and then sat down in the
living room to read the newspaper.

"Sandy," Mrs. Connors asked, "what exactly
are you going to be doing today? Last night you
mentioned something about tracking down Peter
Mullens, but I'm afraid I'm a bit hazy on the details."
She smiled and set down her newspaper. Sandy
explained about the clue in the classified section she,
Betty and the Pinkerton sisters had deciphered the day
before. "We spoke with Officer Murray about it and
he said he would put the word out to the policemen
on patrol last night to speak with the night watchmen
at nearby banks. We're also going to be looking for
Peter Mullens' car." Mrs. Connors nodded.

"That should be an easy task," she said. "It seems
to me that the hard part will be finding out where he
went after the first meeting place."

"Yes," Sandy agreed that would be the challenge.
"I'm hoping that Peter Mullens found some way to
leave a clue, whether he was abducted or left of his
own accord."

"Why would he leave by choice? His wife and
child are here!" Mrs. Connors asked.

"Perhaps he knew they wouldn't be safe while these men were looking for him, so he left hoping the men would follow him and leave his family alone. Or he may have gone looking for them to try to put an end to the problem," Sandy suggested.

"Sandy, dear, I have to say I don't see a man sticking around for a week while he knows his wife and child are in danger, and moreover that his wife is wanted for kidnapping, then suddenly leaving without telling her." Sandy said she felt sure Peter Mullens had not left of his own accord. "I think he was forced to- whether that means he was abducted or threatened in such a way that he genuinely felt he had no choice but to leave, I'm not sure. But I agree, his leaving by choice doesn't fit in with the rest of his actions." She said that part of the reason she wanted to discuss the possibility of his leaving out of free will was to spare Betty and Lisa as much anxiety as possible.

Mrs. Connors shook her head. "The poor woman's husband is missing; whether he left by choice or was kidnapped, the end result is the same: he isn't here, and she doesn't know why. That's going to make her very anxious, no matter what the reason is." Sandy agreed that her mother was undoubtedly right, then said determinedly, "I'm going to find her husband though! Perhaps not today, but I am going to find him!" Mrs. Connors said that was the right spirit, "I'm sure you will find him, dear." At that moment Sandy was surprised to hear a knock on the door. She and her mother exchanged glances and went together to answer it.

Sandy put her eye to the peephole and was again surprised to see a police officer on the step. She opened the door and asked him if there was

a problem. "No, ma'am," he said. He showed the
two women his badge and explained that he was
the officer stationed to watch the house for the early
morning shift. "I'm going off duty now; chief says
there won't be an officer stationed here during the
day so I wanted to let you know before I left. Nothing
untoward occurred last night. The officer stationed
here before me reported no disturbances either. If
you'll be requiring a police watch at this location
again tonight, please call headquarters. Have a good
day, ma'am." The officer touched his hat and turned to
leave.

Sandy and Mrs. Connors were both relieved
that the report had been a positive one. "Some of
your mysteries make me very jumpy, Sandy dear!"
Mrs. Connors said. "Every time a policeman comes
knocking on this door I worry he's got something
terrible to report about a case you're working on!"
Sandy apologized for causing her mother worry. "At
least this time it was unfounded!" she said. At that
moment Betty Mullens came down the stairs, carrying
Lisa. The child looked around with bright, inquisitive
eyes. Mrs. Connors was immediately entranced with
the baby and went to speak with her. Betty gave Lisa
to Sandy's mother and asked if there was any milk for
her. Sandy hastened to the kitchen to prepare some,
heating it up and putting it into a bottle Betty had
brought along. Betty also had some baby food, which
she gave to her daughter. While Lisa was eating, Mrs.
March came down and soon the four women and
the little girl were seated around the dining room
table. Sandy relayed the news that there had been no
disturbances in the night and shared her plan for the
day.

"As soon as the police station is open, I'll call and see what the news is from the banks' night watchmen," Sandy said, glancing at the clock and noting the station would be open in twenty minutes. "I'll call the Pinkerton sisters as well," she said, "and then we go investigate!"

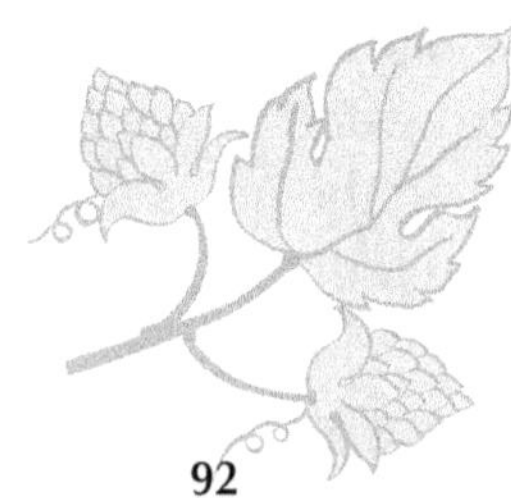

CHAPTER 16

Before Sandy could phone the police station, however, the doorbell rang. Sandy and her mother, still wary of any trouble, went to the door together. Mrs. Connors peeked through the peephole and smiled. "It's Rose and Lily," she told Sandy while unlocking and pulling open the door. "Come in, girls!" She said to the sisters, "You're early; Sandy was just about to phone you!" Lily laughed as she and Rose walked in.

"We didn't want to miss any excitement!" she said. "We also thought that you might want some help cleaning up before we left - our cousins visited a few weeks ago with their baby and boy, do little kids create some big messes!" Rose laughed and agreed, saying she would be happy to help with any dishes. Mrs. Connors thanked the sisters for their help but said that baby Lisa was a very tidy house guest. "Betty brought along her own bottles, but of course I will wash those for her."

"Girls, we have a few minutes still until the police station is open, would you mind helping me fold up the blankets and take the sheets off the guest beds upstairs?" Sandy asked. Rose and Lily agreed and the three quickly accomplished the task. Lily offered to take the folded blankets to the hall closet, saying that she knew Sandy didn't want to waste a minute before phoning the station for news. Sandy grinned and thanked Lily for her offer. Then she hurried to the hall phone. After chatting with the receptionist for a few minutes, Sandy was transferred to Officer Murray, who answered after several rings.

"Good morning, Officer, this is Sandy Connors. I'm calling to check on the news from the night watchmen at the local banks."

"Good morning, Sandy," Officer Murray said. "I've just received and collated all of those reports. We have several banks which had sightings to match the description of the event you gave us."

"Several?" Sandy was surprised. "I didn't imagine Peter Mullens going to multiple places! He can't have had time!"

"If I understand the time line correctly, he didn't have time. I'm sure he didn't go to all these places, but given the somewhat sketchy details we were working with, we can't rule out any of these three locations. I'll give you the location and name of each bank, as well as the pertinent information and I'm sure you'll be able to find out which one is the right one when you visit." He paused a few moments while Sandy got a pencil and a pad of paper. "Ready? All right. The first location is the Allied Bank and Trust in Marinaville. It's directly on the main street. The second location is America Bank in Valley Village. The address is given as 332 Sunset Drive." Sandy said she had a map that included the small town of Valley Village and she would look up the street.

"Okay, I admit I don't know the town of Valley Village very well, so I'm not sure where Sunset Drive is!" Officer Murray laughed. "The third location is further away - it's the Allied Bank and Trust in Headsville, about fifty miles north of here. The bank is on Third Avenue. I personally feel that's further than Peter Mullens would have gone; a fifty mile drive there and back wouldn't leave him very much time to talk, but the description of the car given by the night watchman matched Peter Mullens vehicle, so we've included it. Any other questions?" Sandy said she understood all the locations.

"My friends and I are going to go check them out today. I will call with any information I find. Was the judge able to rescind the warrant on Betty Mullens?"

"Yes," Officer Murray said. "I went to the judge's chambers first thing this morning and the warrant has been taken care of. Betty Mullens is no longer wanted by the Santa Maria police. I presume there were no problems last night?"

"No. The patrolman who was stationed outside this morning checked in before he left and said there was nothing to report. Mrs. March stayed the night with Betty Mullens. Shall I drop her back off at the station before we leave?" Sandy asked.

"I can send a patrolman to pick her up - she won't need to stay any more nights, now that the warrant has been rescinded. "Officer Murray offered. "I'm sure you're eager to begin your search!" Sandy laughed, thanked the officer, hung up and went back to the living room to report to the Pinkertons, Betty and her mother. She saw that Mrs. March had finished her breakfast and was sitting in the living room with the other women. Sandy told them all about what the night watchmen had discovered, reading the addresses of the banks that Officer Murray had given her. "I agree with Officer Murray that the Headsville bank is the least promising; it's so far. But I'm not sure whether the Marinaville or the Valley Village bank is more likely. Both of those towns are about twenty minutes drive. Peter Mullens could easily have gotten there and back and had time for a meeting."

"Sandy, isn't Valley Village a old, scenic village with a large retirement population?" Rose asked. Sandy said she thought it was. "Then I think that's the right one," she continued. "A mostly older population, there isn't likely to be anyone out late at night to disturb the meeting."

"But that could also be a detriment," Lily jumped in. "If there's no one around after dark then any people out late would call a lot of attention to themselves! I think the Marinaville bank is more likely, for that very reason." Sandy agreed that both girls had valid points. She turned to Betty and asked if either place had any significance to her husband that she knew of.

"I'm not sure," she said slowly. "I'm pretty sure Peter has been to Marinaville before. We went once, shortly after we arrived in Santa Maria because the Marinaville kitchen outlet had a particular pan I wanted. We got lost in the outskirts on our way there and Peter seemed to recognize some of the landmarks and found his way into the city after that. I asked him about it and he just said that 'all cities look very much alike.' I don't know quite what that meant, but he seemed not to want to talk about it." Sandy thanked her for sharing.

"I think we should go to Marinaville first. It's possible that Peter had never been there before and the connection may be a coincidence, but still. It's the only link we have." She told Mrs. March that a patrolman would be coming soon to pick her up. She asked Rose and Lily if they were ready to go on a sleuthing expedition, and both girls answered yes. "Sandy?" Betty asked tentatively, "Would you be terribly upset if I didn't go? I want to find my husband, but I also have Lisa to take care of. She's such a good baby, but taking her in the car is quite a bit of trouble. You have all the information you need to find Peter's trail."

Sandy smiled and said that it wouldn't be a problem at all. "I was wondering if you'd like to stay here," she said. "I understand how stressful all this moving about must be for you and Lisa." Mrs. Connors said that she would be happy to have Betty and Lisa stay with her that day. "That baby is just wonderful; it's been a long time since I've had such a little child in my house." The woman smiled at Lisa, who was sitting on the rug playing with a rattle her mother had given her. Sandy rose and bid farewell to her mother, Betty and Lisa. She thanked Mrs. March for her help and went to get the maps of Marinaville and Valley Village. Rose and Lily said goodbye to the other women, too, and soon the three were in Sandy's car, driving towards Marinaville.

In the car on the way they discussed the case. Sandy said she was concerned that Peter Mullens was being held captive. "I just can't imagine his not communicating with his wife if he were free to do so." Rose and Lily agreed. Rose spoke up, saying, "Why are they coming after Peter Mullens now? It's been years since he's been involved in anything criminal!"

"Perhaps they just found him," Lily suggested. Sandy agreed, saying she was sure Peter was now living by the law but that his former associates were out for revenge. "He did leave the gang without permission, remember." Rose agreed it was possible. The three girls discussed other possibilities throughout the drive, until Sandy saw a sign for Marinaville and took the exit.

CHAPTER 17

Sandy turned off the highway at the Marinaville exit. She reminded the girls to keep their eyes open for the Allied Bank and Trust. Sandy was easily able to find Main Street and she drove slowly down the thoroughfare. "This looks like a quiet town," Rose noted, observing that the girls had only passed a few cars as they drove through the downtown area. Sandy agreed. "That would make this an ideal place for Peter Mullens to meet someone in secret," she added. At that moment, Lily pointed out the sign for the Allied Bank and Trust. Sandy turned into the parking lot and selected a space. She suggested the three girls walk around the parking lot first to see if there were any cars that matched Betty's description.

Rose and Lily agreed, and the three quickly walked around the lot; none of them saw a car that matched the description. Sandy noted also that the whole lot was clearly visible from both the Main Street and the bank building itself. "I doubt Peter's associates would have chosen such an exposed location, but perhaps they met here and then drove elsewhere. Officer Murray said the late night watchman reported two cars in the lot just before midnight. He said the lighting was so poor he could not identify make or even color and both vehicles were gone before he was able to come over and speak to them. The watchman claims that on his previous trip around the building there had been no cars in the lot. It was very windy here last night so no one heard the cars."

"So the cars were here only as long as one walk around this building takes. That would mean that Peter and whomever he met would have had, what, two minutes to talk? Maybe less?" Rose asked. Sandy said she was not certain. "The time it would take to walk around would depend on how tall the watchman is and how quickly he walks. It's possible they had up to five minutes, which would have been enough time to talk briefly. The watchman reported that both vehicles were seen in the back right corner of the lot." Sandy gestured to the indicated corner and the three girls walked toward it. Lily noted that there were no marks on the asphalt ground. One of the parking spaces indicated had a green sedan parked there now.

Sandy walked around the sedan, looking for clues. She also searched the ground on either side of the sedan. Rose spoke up, saying, "This green sedan isn't Peter Mullens' car. Perhaps the men he met took his car somewhere and left this one here since they knew no one would recognize it. Peter Mullens may have been kidnapped in his own car!" Sandy agreed that this was possible, but reminded Rose that the watchman had reported both cars driving away. "And there were no cars in the lot this morning when the manager came to open the branch."

"Oh," Rose looked crestfallen. "Then whose car do you think this is?" At that moment a woman in her late fifties came out of the bank and approached the three girls. She was carrying a rather large bag and the girls could see her putting some documents into the bag. She smiled at the girls as she got into the sedan, started the motor and drove away. Rose burst out laughing. "How silly can I be? Here we are in a bank parking lot during business hours and I completely disregard the thought that perhaps this car belongs to a legitimate bank customer! What a joke!" Sandy grinned and said that though Rose's theory had turned out to be wrong, she appreciated the ideas.

"I have to admit I may be grasping at straws with this whole search party. I don't know what I think I'll find. I'm hoping that perhaps Peter Mullens knew he was going to be kidnapped and he had a moment to surreptitiously leave a clue - perhaps a piece of paper or a pen or something discreet that his kidnappers did not notice. Something he left might give Betty a clue or have some meaning for her. Of course, if we do find his car then we may have even more clues." Sandy asked the girls if they would look thoroughly over the ground in all the surrounding spots and the flower beds at the back of the lot. Rose and Lily agreed, and the three spent several minutes combing the ground. None found anything. Sandy sighed, and said that she had to conclude that Peter Mullens had not been to that bank the previous night.

The three girls got back in Sandy's car and soon had begun the drive to Valley Village. She chose to take a country rode which wound throughout the hills to the picturesque town and the girls greatly enjoyed the drive. Once they arrived in the small town, Sandy suggested they stop for a bite to eat and then proceed to the bank. She located a small restaurant with a pretty garden out front and the three girls were soon seated inside. A plump, middle-aged waitress came over to take their order. She introduced herself as Mabel and said she had lived in Valley Village for years and asked the girls what they were doing in town. Momentarily stymied for an answer, Rose and Lily looked at Sandy.

"Oh, we came into town trying to find a book I lost here a few days ago. I came through town and stopped at the bank and a few other places and must have dropped the book out of my car. We're going to head over to the bank after we eat to look around," Sandy quickly explained.

"Well isn't that a funny coincidence," Mabel said. "My husband, Ricky, works as a night watchman at the bank. He does the 9 PM to 6 AM shift and there's never been a single issue until last night, then today here you three come looking for something at that bank! I hope it wasn't a valuable book - there were some men up to no good in the parking lot last night and they may have stolen it!" Sandy hastened to assure the woman that the book had no value except to her. "It's a common volume but it was a gift from my mother." She then adroitly steered the conversation back towards the bank. "I imagine there's very little crime in this small town - what exactly were the men up to?" She asked.

"Well I don't know all that much. Like you say, we don't have much crime here. I've heard as that sometimes kids come into town late at night and park in business lots to smoke or do some drinking, but Ricky has never had a problem with that at that bank. He said that a few cars pulled in and then some people began arguing. He went over to talk to them and one of the guys - these were big, tough looking guys he said, not kids - one of these guys tells him to mind his own business and that they're all leaving soon. Well, it isn't Ricky's job to get into fights with people in the parking lot, so he just tells them they need to leave and then he said he saw two of the tough guys get into one of the cars and a third get into the other. The funny thing was that there was another guy he saw, a meek looking man who got into the car with the third tough guy. Then they all drove off but they left one of their cars! How strange is that?" Mabel shook her head and pulled an order pad out of her pocket.

As Rose and Lily gave their orders, Sandy tried to think of a way to ask about the color of the cars without sounding suspicious, but she couldn't come up with one. She gave Mabel her order for a chicken sandwich and then told the girls what she had been thinking about. Rose reminded Sandy that if they did find any clues to link Peter Mullens' disappearance with the bank here the police could question the watchman again and ask about the car color. "Remember, though, it was night. This town doesn't look like a place that has many strong electric streetlights on at midnight!" Sandy laughed and agreed. She said that was perhaps the exact reason why the men had chosen this town for the meeting. The three continued to discuss the curious incident Mabel had described as they ate their food, and soon were ready to leave. Sandy paid the bill and the three left, after thanking Mabel for the information.

Sandy pulled out of the lot and followed the map to Sunset drive. She saw the bank almost as soon as she turned off the main road and pulled into the lot and parked. As the girls got out of the car, Sandy pointed to a back corner of the lot and said, "This is where the watchman reported the incident, according to Officer Murray's report." There was a dirty white coupe parked in the corner Sandy had indicated, and the three walked over to look at the car.

CHAPTER 18

At first, Sandy was disappointed. Peter Mullens had driven a brown sedan to the meeting. She reminded herself that the man might have taken Mr. Mullens away in his own car, and left behind one of their own. She asked Rose and Lily to walk around the car and the parking lot and look for anything suspicious while she examined the car. First, she went around to the back of the car and wrote down the license plate number. She noted that the car had Illinois plates. "The gang Mr. Mullens used to work with did some work in Chicago," Sandy remembered, elated. She decided to look for more definite clues, however, and walked around the rest of the car.

Sandy reminded herself that she could not open the doors of the vehicle, even if they were unlocked. "The police can tow the car and then examine the inside if it can be tied to Mr. Mullens' disappearance. Now if only I can find something to connect the two!" She continued her circuit around the car, noting that all the tires were heavily worn and covered in an odd, reddish mud. "I wonder if the mud came from somewhere around here or if the car picked it up on the drive out from Chicago. I don't know of any place locally that has dirt of that color!" Sandy concluded that the mud had come from somewhere further east and wondered how she could use it to find the kidnapped man. Deciding she should focus now on examining the rest of the car, she turned her attention away from the tires. She looked inside the windows of the vehicle but was unable to see anything, aside from a few scattered papers and a man's rain hat on the back seat. She squinted at the papers, using her hands to shield the glare of the sun from the window, but she was unable to read anything.

At that moment, Rose and Lily returned. Rose said she had found some evidence of a scuffle at the edge of the parking lot. "I saw of lot of mixed up footprints, and some plants looked trampled and there's a broken tree branch," she explained, pointing to a place on the edge of the lot a few spots further down. Sandy said she would like to see the area for herself, explaining that she had found some clues. She told the sisters about the mud, the license plate, and mentioned the papers inside. "I can't read any of them," she said with a sigh, "but I hope the police will have enough evidence to tow the car and open it so we can find out what they say."

The three girls now walked to the footprints Rose had found and Sandy looked closely at the area. She agreed with Rose's interpretation that there had been a struggle of some sort. "It's hard to identify specific footprints; they're so mixed up. I'm sure, however, that there were at least three people involved. You can see here, at the edge, a very clear man's shoe print made by a heavyset man in rubber soled tennis shoes." She pointed to the print, and then gestured to a different print at the other end of the morass. "This print here, also of the right foot, was clearly made by a much slighter man, also wearing rubber soled shoes. And here in the middle of the mess of prints, you can see a partial impression from a pair of dress shoes. So unless one of the men was wearing a mismatched pair of shoes, this had to have come from yet another man." Sandy paused for a second, musing.

"Sandy, what are you thinking?" Lily asked, "I
know that look well enough by now!" Sandy laughed
and said that an idea had occurred to her, but it was
a wild one. "If Betty happens to remember either her
husband's shoe size or the type of shoes he wore, we
might be one step closer to proving that he was here!
You'll note that the print from the shoe at the back
- from the heavyset fellow - indicates a very large
shoe. This print, I would guess came from a very tall,
heavy man. If Peter Mullens is such a man, we have
one more clue that he could have been here." Rose
laughed, saying she thought Sandy might be reaching
a bit far.

"Perhaps," Sandy conceded. "I never did ask Betty
for a physical description of her husband, though; just
for his car. I didn't imagine we would find him at any
of the banks today! As soon as we get home, I will ask
her for a description of him." Sandy laughed, adding
that she would ask Betty about her husband's shoes
and their soles, but said that she did not think it likely
the woman knew anything about that. "Most people
pay more attention to the top of the shoe than the
soles, although the soles of shoes can give you some
very interesting information."

"Really?" Lily asked, interested. She pressed Sandy
to tell the girls more about the imprints at which they
were looking. Sandy obliged, and, carefully avoiding
confusing the mess of prints anymore, stepped closer
to the area. She studied all the prints carefully for a
minute. "This is why I think this print at the rear was
made by a tall man - not just the shoe size. You can
just see in between the plants here a matching left
print. I believe they were made when he stood here -
you can see that they are quite far apart. A man would

have to have long legs to leave prints that far apart.
I would also guess that the slighter man came over,
walking across the plants, from the parking spot with
the white coupe. I would guess that he's one of the
criminals."

Rose and Lily were amazed. "Sandy, that's
incredible! I could never have gotten all that
information from a few mixed up prints!" Rose
burst out. Sandy smiled and waved off the praise,
saying she was merely using logic and making a few
educated guesses. She then gestured to the dress shoe
imprint near the front. "I would guess that this man
came from a car which was parked in this spot right in
front of the prints. He was met by the tall man at the
back and they were soon joined by the third man."
She detected a line of partial prints made by the slight
man in rubber soled shoes coming diagonally up to
the large grouping of prints. Showing them to Rose
and Lily, she said, "I would guess that this man came
running up from a car in the middle spot, or perhaps
he was just standing in that area. The fact that he left
only the front part of prints indicates he was running,
sprinting really, for the short distance across the
planted area. Also, note how this print in the middle
of the group is fairly deep - it would seem he did
something that put much more weight on his shoes
than normal at that point.

"Now, that's about all I can tell from the prints
but those facts suggest a story. I would guess that
Peter Mullens parked in this spot here," Sandy
began, indicating the spot where Rose and Lily were
standing. "Then, as he got out of his car, he spoke
with the tall man in back for a while - I can't tell how

long - and Peter then turned to go. That's when the slighter man dashed up, pulled Peter onto the dirt border and the scuffle began. Perhaps he dragged or carried Peter Mullens to a car. That would explain why there's no set of prints matching the dress shoes."

"How did the tall man get back to any of the cars?" Rose asked, indicating that there was no return set of prints for him either. Sandy admitted that it also puzzled her. "Perhaps he walked across the plants on his way back to the car, so no prints were left," Lily suggested. Sandy admitted that was possible, but added also that she could have interpreted the prints incorrectly. "We will have to wait until Peter Mullens is found, or his kidnappers are caught, before we can determine exactly what happened." Sandy paused for a moment. "If, in fact, this is where Peter Mullens was kidnapped. We have a lot of evidence that points to it, but nothing that proves it! Perhaps another interview with the night watchman will tell more." She sighed, and then asked if Lily had found anything of interest.

"Well, I did find a few things, though I'm not sure how much you'll be interested in them." She pulled a button from her pocket and a scrap of newspaper. "I found this button on the other side of the lot - it's clean so I don't think it's been out there too long. And this piece of newspaper was also across the lot, tangled in the bushes. It's also clean and dry. It rained hard two nights ago so I would guess it hasn't been here for that long." Sandy took the items from Lily and examined them.

"I'm sure you're right about the timing. This button still has some threads in it that have been ripped - it must have gotten ripped off of someone's coat recently. And girls!" Sandy became quite excited. "This is a scrap of paper from the Santa Maria Gazette! It's ripped from the classified ads, and I think it was taken from the ad right above the one Peter Mullens' enemies placed in the paper day before yesterday!"

CHAPTER 19

Sandy was elated - this was surely the clue necessary to prove that Peter Mullens had been kidnapped from this very spot! She commended Lily on finding the things and commented that she was sure the wind had blown them across the parking lot into the plants on the other side. Rose and Lily agreed. Sandy said she wanted to look around the lot one more time before they left, though she felt there was nothing more to be learned from the area. "I would like to report all we've learned to the police this afternoon; after we speak to them, perhaps they will be able to tow this car before the criminals come back for it. We should also ask the night watchman a few more questions, but that can wait until tomorrow."

As soon as Sandy had finished explaining this to the Pinkerton sisters, she began to walk around the edge of the parking lot, looking carefully for any other footprints or scraps of paper. She completed a circuit around the lot without seeing anything, however, and soon the three girls were heading back to Santa Maria in Sandy's car. She drove directly to the police station, saying she would phone her house from there and ask Betty about the button and her husband's shoes. "I don't want to make her take Lisa downtown any more than is necessary; I'm sure that going anywhere with such a young child is a complicated procedure!" Rose and Lily agreed, saying that any information Sandy needed from Betty could surely be obtained by phone.

Presently, Sandy pulled into the Santa Maria Police station parking lot. She locked her car, and the three girls went into the building, Lily holding onto the scrap of newspaper and the button tightly. Fortunately Officer Murray was available to speak to the girls, and soon they had told the entire story. He took notes about the deductions Sandy had made from the footprints and wrote down the license plate number. Next, the girls showed him the button and the newspaper scrap. Sandy again explained what she was sure they meant, and Officer Murray agreed. Sandy then mentioned that she wanted to phone Betty Mullens at her own home and ask her a few questions. Officer Murray directed her to a phone she could use and she quickly put in the call.

Sandy's mother answered the phone, and after chatting for a few moments, Sandy asked to speak to Betty. She assured her mother that she and the girls would be home soon and she would tell her the whole story at that time. Betty was soon on the phone, saying that Lisa was taking a nap. Sandy told the women briefly what they had discovered, adding that she had a few questions for her. "Betty, do you remember what your husband was wearing when he went to meet his former associates?" Sandy asked.

"He was wearing a tan suit and an overcoat. It was windy that night, I remember, so he wore his thick coat. It's long, and dark brown," Betty described.

"Does it have buttons?" Sandy queried.

"Yes, it does," Betty answered after thinking for a moment. "It's a double breasted wool coat with large brown buttons down the front. Sandy, why are you wondering about my husband's coat?"

"We found a button that looked like it had been ripped off of a coat on the ground of one of the parking lots. I wanted to know if it might be from your husband's coat. I have just one more question for you," Sandy said. "Do you remember anything about your husband's shoes?" Betty thought for a minute. "I think he was wearing dress shoes. Brown, with laces and smooth leather soles." Sandy thanked her, and assured her that she had been very helpful. "We will be home shortly and will tell you the entire story. Thanks again for the help!" Sandy then returned to speak with Officer Murray.

"Betty Mullens said her husband wore a dark brown wool overcoat with buttons the night he disappeared. I think it's likely that this button came from his coat, and the prints of the man in dress shoes could well be Peter's." Sandy now told the officer about the papers that she had seen in the abandoned car. "Is there enough evidence to tow the car and examine the inside?" She asked.

"Most likely there is," Officer Murray said. "I'm going to check this license plate number against a listing of stolen or abandoned vehicles. If it matches any listed cars it should certainly be towed. I will take care of that right now and let you know tomorrow if we have the car here at the station." Sandy thanked the officer, then the three girls left, leaving the button and scrap of newspaper with him to add to the case file.

Within a few minutes, Sandy had arrived at her home. She asked Rose and Lily if they wanted to stay for dinner. "I want to tell Mom, Dad and Betty what we found out today." Rose said she would phone her parents and ask; soon she had received permission for her and Lily to stay. The three girls said hello to Betty and Mrs. Connors and then went to set the table with extra places.

Soon, Mr. Connors came home from work; he kissed his wife and daughter and said hello to Rose, Lily and Betty. He was pleased to hear that the Pinkerton sisters would be staying for dinner. Sandy helped her mother to drain a pot of potatoes and removed a roasting pan of chicken from the oven. She dished the meat onto plates, adding potatoes and carrots from a sauté pan. The food was quickly brought to the table and everyone declared the meal delicious. Sandy began to tell the story of the discoveries the girls made that day, adding that they had not been to the third possible bank, but she felt sure they found the site of Mr. Mullens kidnapping.

She began by relating what Mabel, the waitress at the luncheon spot, had told the girls about her husband's job as a night watchman. "As soon as I heard that story, I began to suspect that the bank in Valley Village would be where we would find evidence of his kidnapping. We went to the bank directly after lunch and saw the abandoned car still in the lot. It was a white coupe with Illinois plates; I'm fairly certain that it belongs to one of Mr. Mullens kidnappers!" Sandy told about the strange mud on the tires, the papers inside the car that she couldn't read and her deductions about the footprints in the dirt. Betty smiled when she heard this, "That's why you wondered what the tread of Peter's shoes is, isn't it?" The woman shook her head, "I'm sorry I don't know but I'm not terribly observant about details like that!" Sandy smiled and said that most people would not know the tread of their own shoes. "I didn't expect you to know, but I thought I would ask, in case you had happened to notice at some point."

Sandy then told the others about the button and newspaper clipping which Lily had discovered. "Fortunately, you did remember what kind of coat your husband was wearing so I feel certain when I say the button came from his coat. It must have gotten ripped off during the struggle; fallen to the ground and rolled across the lot. The newspaper clipping likely blew out of a car - either your husband's, or the kidnappers'. They both could have had a copy of that paper with them. It blew across the lot and got caught in the bushes near the button. We gave all this information to Officer Murray, who is going to check out the vehicle and have it towed to the police station if possible," the young sleuth finished her narrative.

"Sandy, I can't thank you enough for going to all this effort to find my husband," Betty said. She began to say something else, but presently she heard Lisa crying in the other room and excused herself to take care of her daughter. Once Betty had left, Mr. Connors also congratulated Sandy on her deductions. "What do you plan to do next?" he asked.

"I'm hoping Officer Murray will be able to tow the car; then I'll examine the papers inside and perhaps they will provide a clue. I may also track down the source of the reddish mud that was on the tires." Her father commended her for these ideas, and the rest of the meal was spent discussing other matters. Soon after, Sandy drove Rose and Lily home and the family retired for the night.

CHAPTER 20

The next morning Sandy was up early. She hoped that Officer Murray had been able to tow the white coupe from the bank parking lot and there would be clues inside! Sandy went downstairs and breakfasted with her mother and father. Halfway through the meal, the telephone rang. Sandy excused herself to answer it, hoping it would be Officer Murray. "Hello?" She said as she picked up the handset. There was silence on the other end for several seconds. Sandy had just begun to think that the connection had been interrupted when a deep male voice began to speak.

"Give up searching for Peter Mullens if you don't want to get hurt!" Then the caller hung up! Sandy stood lost in thought for several minutes. She had not recognized the voice and the man gave no identifying details. "I wonder if he was trying to disguise his voice," she mused. "It sounded artificially low." Presently Sandy's mother called to her daughter, asking who had been on the line. Sandy returned to the breakfast room and told her parents what had happened. Mrs. Connors was aghast. "Why, dear, those men may be waiting to hurt you! I think you should give up working on this case!" Mr. Connors was also upset, but less so than his wife.

"If they are becoming upset now, I think it means you're on the right track. I feel Sandy will be safe enough working in connection with the police and with Rose and Lily." He spoke directly to his daughter, "I think you should be extremely careful - please don't go anywhere by yourself and keep both your mother and me well informed of where you are planning to go." Sandy agreed with the precautions and assured both her parents she would be very careful. "I don't plan to let these villains get away with kidnapping Peter Mullens! I am going to find them, and free Mr. Mullens!"

"That's the spirit, Sandy!" Her father commended her, "Don't let the bad guys win!" Sandy smiled and said she would phone the Santa Maria police right after breakfast to report the call. The trio began to talk of lighter topics and soon the meal was finished. Sandy helped her mother clear and wash the plates while her father got ready for work and kissed him goodbye as he left. She then placed a call to the police station. She was told that Officer Murray was not available at that moment, but she left a message for him, asking him to return the call as soon as he had a chance. "I wonder where he could be," the young detective mused. "Perhaps he's out working on something related to the white car."

She returned to the kitchen and found Betty awake and downstairs with Lisa. She helped the woman mix and heat up some formula for the child's breakfast and as Lisa was eating, she told Betty about the phone call. Sandy tried to make light of the matter, but Betty became quite upset. "Sandy, I don't want you to get hurt for my family! These men are very bad guys!" Sandy assured Betty that she would take every precaution. "I will report the call to Officer Murray the next time we speak; he's not at the station at this moment. I hope he's working on towing the car from the bank lot back to Santa Maria so we can examine it."

Betty said she was still concerned and begged the young woman to be careful. Sandy continued to reassure her that she would take no unnecessary risks as the two washed out Lisa's bottles and wiped down the counters. Betty then made herself a quick breakfast and Sandy took Lisa in to the living room and played with the girl while her mother ate. Betty had just finished breakfast and returned to take her daughter back when the phone rang. Sandy answered it, hoping this time it would be Officer Murray. She was pleased to hear the policeman identify himself. He asked first why Sandy had phoned. She explained about the threatening call, saying she thought the man had tried to disguise his voice. "It was abnormally low and sounded forced," she explained.

Officer Murray took several notes about the call, then said, "There isn't much to go on there. We will trace the call as well as we can, but the message was so short and you say there were no identifying features, beyond the disguised voice?"

"Well ..." Sandy thought deeply for a minute. "There was some noise in the background, very faint, but it sounded like birds and trees rustling. There were no horns or car noises at all. So perhaps he was calling from somewhere rural." Officer Murray wrote these observations down as well. Then Sandy asked him about the car and he said it was being towed as they spoke. "I'm expecting it to arrive to the station by mid morning. Shall I call you once it is here and you can go through the papers with me? Any forensic work on the car will have to be done in the lab, which I'm afraid you can't enter as a private citizen, but we can take the papers you saw out of the vehicle before it goes to the lab." Sandy thanked the man for the offer and said she would very much appreciate a chance to look over the papers. She then said goodbye.

Sandy put in a call to the Pinkertons, explaining what had happened and asking them to come over to her house. "I have a hunch I would like to work on before we get called to the station!" Rose and Lily said they would be over soon, and Sandy went to tell Betty, excusing herself for a few moments to get some books she thought would be helpful. By the time she returned to the living room, the Pinkerton sisters had arrived. The four women were chatting and playing with Lisa, who seemed pleased to be the center of attention.

Sandy came in with a pile of books and explained her idea. "I noticed some red mud on the tires of the white coupe, then when the man called this morning I heard in the background noises like one would hear in the woods - bird song and trees blowing in the breeze. I originally thought the mud had gotten onto the car sometime during the drive from Illinois to California, but now I'm thinking that perhaps the gang's hideout is somewhere in the woods, near enough to get to and from the Valley Village Bank in one night and have the Santa Maria Paper available. So I brought these books about local geology and natural areas. I think we should go through them, focusing on isolated areas with little supervision and see if any place looks like it might match those features!"

Lily commented, "There are a lot of wooded areas around here and that's a pretty wide radius!"

"I agree, it's a slim clue, but that reddish mud was so strange looking, and there was so much of it caked onto the tires that now I'm sure the car hadn't been driven all the way across the country since it picked up the mud. I don't know of any area around here with mud like that, so we should probably focus on places which are close-by but not in the immediate vicinity of Santa Maria." Sandy distributed the books to the Pinkerton sisters and Betty; her mother took Lisa into the dining room to play peekaboo while the others worked.

There was silence in the room for some time as each girl skimmed through the contents of one of the books. Sandy was the first to reach the end of her book, having found nothing about red dirt. She picked up a second book and began to look through it. She had barely opened the book when she heard Betty give a gasp of surprise. "What is it?" Sandy asked, coming to her side. Betty pointed to a paragraph in the book, which was about the geological climate in the town of Valley Village. Sandy saw that red dirt was found in the hills just outside the town! She shared Betty's findings with Rose and Lily, who were stunned.

Lily spoke first, "Well that makes a lot of sense! They have their hideout right by the meeting place!"

"It does make a lot of sense." Sandy agreed. "We will have to go out there as soon as we're through examining the car. I hope Officer Murray calls soon!"

CHAPTER 21

Sandy had just expressed a wish for news when the phone rang. She excused herself and stepped into the hallway to answer the phone. It was, in fact, Officer Murray, who said the white coupe had just arrived at the downtown police station. "Would you and your friends like to come down and look at the papers? Our locksmith is working on door; it should only be a few moments before he has it open." Sandy thanked the officer for calling and said she would be down to the station soon.

"I think we've found a clue to the location of the gang's hideout!" Sandy said. "I would prefer to discuss it with you in person, at the station." Sandy told Rose, Lily, Betty and her mother, who was still holding baby Lisa, that the car had arrived at the station. "Who wants to come with me to examine the papers?" she asked. Both Rose and Lily immediately said they wanted to come along. Betty hesitated.

"I want to help find my husband - of course I want to help," she said, "but I also want to take good care of my daughter. I'm not sure that the car shop of a local police department would be a very safe place for her."

"Let me take Lisa," Mrs. Connors offered. "I would love to spend a few hours with her!" Betty thanked her, saying that she appreciated the help very much. Sandy agreed it was a good plan. "Betty, there may be things written on these papers that we don't understand but perhaps you'll recognize some from hearing Peter mention them. We won't be gone very long; perhaps two hours at the most." Betty went to show Mrs. Connors where Lisa's formula and diapers were kept and Sandy tidied the pile of books in the living room. She tucked the one in which Betty had found the clue under her arm, thinking, "I had better show this to Officer Murray!" Soon the group was ready to go and Sandy drove directly to the police station.

They made their way inside and found Officer Murray. He led them into the usual room and gestured to a large pile of papers on the table. "These were all taken from the car. If any more are found during the forensic investigation, they will be brought in here as well. Before we begin going through the papers, I have the results back from the license plate search on the white coupe. The car was - and still is - registered to a Chicago citizen - Mr. Theophilous Parker. The car has never been reported stolen or tampered with. Mr. Parker has owned the car for the past eight years; he purchased it new from a local dealership."

"Goodness!" Sandy said, surprised. "I was sure it was going to be a stolen car!"

"Well, there is a mystery about it," Officer Murray continued. "Theophilous Parker passed away eight months ago!"

"Eight months ago!" Betty interjected. "Then who's driving his car now?"

"That's the mystery!" Officer Murray went on to explain. "Mr. Parker had no close family members living when he passed and he left no will. Several members of his extended family have put in claims to his estate. The case will be heard in court several months from now. During the interim time the possessions and assets have been frozen, under the watch of the local police department. Cases like this, however, are rarely a top priority and I doubt that his possessions have been checked on more than one time since his passing. The articles and assets are itemized, so the car should be on the list but it's quite possible no one has noticed it missing. It could have been taken months ago!"

"That's logical," Sandy said, then she grinned, "I wonder how Mr. Theophilous Parker feels about the fact that his car is now being used by criminals?" The others in the room laughed. Sandy then pulled the book out and opened to the page where Betty had read about the mud. She showed the paragraph to Officer Murray, explaining why it was a logical hiding place. Officer Murray agreed, and noted several facts about the mud and the listed locations. The five then began to look through the papers, after Sandy suggested that any phrases they came across that did not make sense should be shown to Betty. "Perhaps you will recognize some of them and be able to connect them to the gang your husband used to work with."

"I'll try," the woman said, sounding a bit dubious, "but there's a good chance I won't recognize all the clues. I'm not a detective, and my husband kept much of the specifics of his criminal life to himself, partly for my own protection."

"Please don't be nervous!" Sandy reassured the woman. "We really already know that this car is used by the men who abducted your husband, we're just looking for any other clues and there's a chance something will seem familiar to you that the rest of us might miss." Sandy smiled and put a hand on Betty's arm for a moment, then the five turned back to the piles of paper in front of them. There was silence in

the room for some minutes, as each person scanned
the documents in front of them. Sandy looked over
a pile of what appeared to be bank statements and
other such financial documents. She looked for
identifying details but saw, to her discouragement,
that the statements did not include names and only
listed the last four digits of each account.

Sandy was about to put the papers aside when she
noticed that there were account listings from several
banks. She looked through them again, paying close
attention to the specific bank and type of account and
was startled to notice that each statement was for a
different account! She counted and discovered that
there were statements for thirteen separate accounts
at four major national banks. She looked up and saw
that the other four were also paying close attention
to the papers. Soon everyone was finished and Sandy
asked what each had found.

Rose spoke up first. "I think these are credit card
statements, but they seem to be for all different cards.
If I've figured this right, there are nine cards here!
The statements are all from the past seven months. I
can't find a name or anything, though there are the
last digits of the card and perhaps with a warrant you
could get the names from the banks," Rose said to
Officer Murray. He said he would look into it, and
then held up his pile of papers and said they were
hotel bills, gas receipts and restaurant bills. "I will
cross check these with the credit card statements, see
if they match." He said, nodding towards the pile of
papers Rose had.

"You'll want these, too," Lily said. "As far as
I can figure, they're also credit card statements
from the past six or seven months. I don't know

if they're different cards than the ones Rose has."
Officer Murray again said he would cross check the
statements. Betty was next, saying that the papers
she had were from a medical file. "There's no name
anywhere on any of the documents - though see here
in this corner where a piece has been ripped off?"
She showed the group a torn corner of one of the
papers. "I would guess the man's name was there and
he removed it. I'm no doctor, but from these papers it
looks like the man had a chronic medical condition
and probably always had the papers with him when
he traveled." Officer Murray said he would have the
police doctor look over the file.

"I will also try to trace a man with this particular
condition through Chicago area hospitals. Perhaps
that will give us his name. Sandy, what do you have?"

"Bank statements. For thirteen accounts at four
different banks!" She held up the pile. "Again, there
are no names anywhere on any of these statements,
but there is account information that can be used to
identify the owner of the accounts with a warrant."
She showed the numbers to Officer Murray and he
nodded, saying he would look into getting a warrant
to trace the owner of the accounts. He piled all the
paper back together neatly, clipping each of the kinds
of papers together into groups. As the women got
ready to leave, Lily spoke up. "Why would a criminal
leave these papers in his car? Surely he would know
that someone could find out who he is from all these
papers?"

CHAPTER 22

Officer Murray responded to Lily's question, saying that criminals sometimes become complacent. "Particularly if they've been successfully evading police for a long time - as this gang has been for almost twenty years - they begin to think they are invincible and get sloppy. Often, this is what leads to catching a criminal. It could also be that whichever member of the gang brought these records is in charge of keeping track of the accounts and felt that leaving the papers behind would be more of a risk." He flipped through some of the papers. "Someone using a bank for personal finance doesn't have this many accounts. Perhaps these are from a legal corporation, but I think it's much more likely that there's some sort of bank fraud going on here. I will call in another officer who works on cases involving financial fraud, and see what he says. I will speak with police in Illinois, too, and see if there are any outstanding warrants for someone connected with crimes like this. If I find a name or description of anyone, I will let you know. Also, anything the forensic team turns up on the car."

Sandy thanked the man, and then the four girls left the station. Sandy drove back to her house, saying that she wanted to go out and investigate the area described in the book with the red mud but felt the girls should set up a more concrete plan first. Betty begged off from the investigation, saying that she wanted to spend the afternoon with her daughter and didn't think it would be safe for Lisa to be out in an area where there were likely to be criminals. Sandy agreed, and soon Betty and her daughter were happily playing together in the Connors' living room. Mrs. Connors said she had read a few storybooks to Lisa before the child fell asleep for a morning nap. "She's a darling little girl, so quiet and calm!"

"Yes," Betty agreed, "she is my little angel. Peter always used to say that she had my temperament - he says he was a feisty child and rarely listened to adults." Betty fell silent and Sandy could see that she was very worried about her husband. Sandy seated herself next to Betty and put an arm around her shoulders. "Please try not to worry; we will find your husband soon, I am sure." Betty smiled wanly and thanked Sandy for the effort.

"Betty," Rose said suddenly, "you said that you and your husband came out here several months ago and thought you were safe. How did the gang find you?"

"I don't know. We were living with Peter's friend - someone whom I gathered he knew from his criminal days, but I don't know for certain - and until he died we weren't bothered. It was quite shortly after his death that we began to get threatening notes, actually."

"I wonder if the gang heard about his death somehow and that led to the discovery that you were staying with him?" Rose mentioned her opinions.

"That is possible," Sandy said, thoughtfully. "Was his obituary published nationally?"

"I don't know. We were subscribing only to the Santa Maria paper, which did feature an obituary and a photo from the funeral. Peter was in the photo, but it was a small picture and it only showed the side of his head. I didn't imagine that anyone could possibly have identified him from it."

"That's an interesting point. I wonder if the Santa Maria library has a copy of the paper we could look at. I hadn't thought about how exactly the gang had tracked you down, but it's possible that they had followed your steps well enough to know you had come to the west coast somewhere and then came across the picture in the paper. It could also be a coincidence that they found you right after your friend passed away. You continued to stay in his house after his death?" Sandy asked.

"Yes," Betty confirmed. "Mark - that was Peter's friend's name - set it up so we were his tenants through next year. We paid him a very slight rent so that everything was legal. Management of the lease was turned over to a local leasing company after Mark's death and we paid rent to them. I gather that the leasing company put money into Mark's trust account. I admit that I didn't pay very close attention to the specifics of the system, however. I signed my name to the lease, as did Peter, but I was pregnant at the time and was setting up a nursery for the baby. Of course, before she was born we began to receive threats and so Lisa didn't get to use the lovely nursery. She did stay there the week after I took her from the Webbers," Betty explained.

Sandy was interested in Betty's story. She had not thought much about how the Mullens had been found, but now she was curious. "I suppose criminals have access to many sources of information that law abiding citizens don't. The fact that it took the gang nearly six months to find you indicates that you did a very good job of covering your trail," Sandy said. "Once we find the criminals, I'll ask them how they found you. Perhaps it was just coincidental timing."

Betty agreed that was possible, then asked the girls how they were planning to search for the red mud. Sandy said she would go back to the Valley Village bank and ask the night watchman a few questions. "It's possible he remembers seeing from which direction the cars turned into the lot, or where they went after they left. If so, I'll follow that direction to the nearby woods and look for hidden roads or trails with muddy tracks. I'm hoping we'll find a small cabin or abandoned car or some other hiding place where the criminals might be. We might even find your husband!"

Betty looked very hopeful at that thought. She thanked Sandy for putting so much thought and effort into finding her husband. "I'm sure you'll succeed!" She praised the young detective.

"Don't praise me too highly until I do succeed!" Sandy said. "I will try as hard as I can, but I can't promise to be successful." Betty smiled and said she understood. She excused herself to put Lisa down for her afternoon nap. Sandy turned to Rose and Lily and outlined her plan in more detail. At that moment the doorbell rang. Sandy stepped into the hallway to answer the door. She put her eye to the peephole but could not see anyone outside. Afraid of trouble, her mother joined her in the hallway. Together, the two women opened the door a crack and looked out. Seeing no one, Sandy opened the door and stepped onto the porch. There was no one there!

She looked around the front yard, porch and down the driveway. There was no one in sight. Curious why the bell was rung, Sandy searched for clues. She saw prints in the soft dirt near the base of the steps that indicated someone had quickly run across the lawn after descending the steps. Sandy followed the prints through the flower bed and saw daubs of mud going down the driveway. "Someone certainly did ring the bell, then ran away on purpose," she said. "The prints continue down the drive to the sidewalk, then stop. He must have gotten into a car here. I didn't hear a car drive away after the bell rang. Did anyone else?" she asked her mother and the Pinkerton sisters, who had followed her out of the house. All three shook their heads no.

"I rarely hear a car on the street from inside the house," Mrs. Connors said. "The house is set far enough back from the road that only very old or loud cars can be heard."

"So we can guess whoever rang the bell drove off in a new, well maintained car," Lily said. Sandy agreed, adding that she felt sure the car had been driven by someone else, and the man who rang the bell jumped in and the driver immediately sped off. "Of course, there was more time than usual for him to get away after he rang the bell since Mother and I opened the door so cautiously," Sandy said. She walked back up to the flower bed and examined the footprints in more detail. "I'm sure these prints were made by a man wearing the same pair of shoes we saw in the mess of prints outside the bank." She pointed to Rose and Lily, who agreed that it did appear to match the prints they had seen at the bank. "I wonder why they rang the bell." She mused. Suddenly Rose gasped.

"What if they rang the bell to get us out of the house and then accomplices broke in the back to kidnap Betty and Lisa?" All four women were alarmed by the idea and ran into the house, hoping that Betty and Lisa were still safe!

CHAPTER 23

Sandy reached the house first. She recalled that Betty had said she was going to put Lisa down for an afternoon nap, so she dashed up the stairs to the guest bedroom. Pushing open the door, she saw that all of the pair's clothes and things were still arrayed around the room, but neither the woman nor the baby were in sight. She called down the stairs to Rose and Lily, "there's no one up here. Are they downstairs?" She ran down the stairs before anyone had a chance to answer and found the Pinkertons in the living room. "There's no one here," Rose said glumly. "I checked the kitchen and study, and Lily checked dining room. Your mother is upstairs now, looking." At that moment, Mrs. Connors came downstairs.

"Are they up there?" Sandy asked.

"No," Mrs. Connors said, looking thoughtful. "There's one more place we should check, though. Follow me." The woman led the way to the back door, explaining that when she had a hard time putting Sandy down for a nap, she would often take her outside to play in the sunshine for a few minutes. "It worked wonders for getting you to take a nap, perhaps Betty has found the same thing with darling Lisa." With some sense of renewed hope, the trio of girls followed Mrs. Connors out into the yard. All four breathed a sigh of relief when they saw Betty and Lisa, sitting in the shade of a fruit tree at the back of the yard. Betty was reading aloud to her child from a storybook.

"Hello!" Betty called, and Lisa waved a pudgy fist in greeting. The four trooped over to the woman and

Sandy told the story of the doorbell, the footprints and the frantic search for them. "Oh no," Betty said, "I'm so sorry to cause so much trouble!" Rose laughed and assured her that the four jumped to conclusions and in no way blamed Betty for the worry. "Besides, you're safe and sound, so is Lisa, so there's nothing to worry about now!" Mrs. Connors explained how she happened to have remembered taking Sandy out into the back yard when she didn't want to take a nap.

"So I thought we should check out here! I'm glad I remembered that!" The woman said.

"I'm glad, also," Betty said. "Lisa didn't want to lay down so I read her a story that usually makes her sleepy; but when she still couldn't fall asleep, I thought a little sunshine would be good for her ... for both of us, actually. Poor Lisa's been so cooped up inside recently." Betty's brow creased with worry and Sandy was sure that the woman was concerned about her husband. She said with renewed vigor, "Girls, let's get going on our search expedition! Valley Village is some miles from here and I want as many hours as possible to look for the gang's hideout!" Rose and Lily agreed, and quickly jumped up from where they sat on the Connors' back lawn.

Sandy's mother said she would stay home with Betty and Lisa, and asked if the three girls were planning to be back in time for dinner. Sandy assured her mother they would, and after saying goodbye to Betty and her toddler, the three soon were in Sandy's car driving toward the town of Valley Village.

Sandy asked Lily to reread the relevant paragraphs out loud from the book on geography as she drove. Lily complied, and soon reached the end of the section. "There's not very much information," Rose said, "nor does the book feature a map of Valley Village. How will we find these areas of red clay?" Sandy said she was concerned about the same thing. "I guess we'll have to drive to several areas near the town and see if we can find any dirt that looks like the red mud from the tires."

"Sandy," Lily spoke up suddenly, closing the book she had set on her lap, "why don't we go back to the restaurant we went to the first time? The waitress, what was her name ... Marie? Marlene?"

"Mabel!" Rose interjected.

"Yes! Mabel!" Lily continued. "She said she's lived in Valley Village all her life. If anyone knows about the geography near the town, she will."

"That's a marvelous idea!" Sandy said. "We can stop for lunch and ask her about hiking areas with red mud near the town. I'm sure people come to the town frequently for the interesting geology, so it won't seem out of place. Good job, Lily!" Sandy smiled at her friend in the front seat. The rest of the drive was quickly accomplished and it was just past noon when the three arrived at the restaurant. Sandy was pleased to see that Mabel was again at work, and she asked the hostess if her party could be seated at a table where Mabel would be their waitress. The request was honored, and soon the three were perusing the menu. Mabel came by soon after they had been seated, and after only a moment, recognized them from before.

"Why, bless me, I know you three! Did you find the book you lost?" She asked

"Yes, we were able to find what we were looking for," Sandy said, smiling at the chatty waitress. She hoped Mabel would ask the girls about their plans that day as a way of steering the conversation toward the red dirt. She was not disappointed as Mabel asked them, "And what brings you back to Valley Village this afternoon? Surely you didn't lose another book!"

"No, no," Sandy laughed. "We noticed the beautiful wooded areas around the town when we were here before and we thought the hiking nearby must be wonderful. I happen to be interested in geology, and I've heard that there are some areas of reddish rocks and dirt nearby. Do you happen to know of any of them?" Mabel thought a minute then replied. She pointed her finger toward the west, and said, "There are some spots with red dirt over that direction. I think there are some hiking trails over that way too, though I don't get out hiking much anymore!" She laughed, and then gave Sandy directions to the area she meant. "It's easy to get there, just follow Main Street all the way down to where it dead ends into the rural highway. Turn west; follow it for about a mile, then you should see signs to a trail head parking lot. I'm sure there are some other hiking trails off of that highway, too."

"Thank you, Mabel," Sandy said, jotting down the directions the woman had given her on a pad of paper from her purse. The three girls then ordered lunch, which was delicious. While the girls were eating, Sandy explained her plan. "I think we should drive out to the trail head, like we're going to go hiking, only let's all keep our eyes open for small, rural roads or driveways branching off of the highway. If we see any dirt roads, we'll take them and see where we wind up. A small cabin or abandoned house off of a rural highway sounds like a perfect place for Peter Mullens' kidnappers to be hiding!" Rose and Lily agreed, and the three quickly finished their meal.

Sandy paid, again thanking Mabel for the information, and the three were soon driving down Main Street.

Sandy turned onto the rural highway, which was a rutted, two-lane road. There was no traffic in either direction. "This certainly is rural!" she laughed, as the car bounced over potholes and cracks in the pavement. "Remember to look for small side roads," she reminded Rose and Lily. She had driven only a few hundred feet when Lily pointed to a side road going up towards the hills, away from town. "That might be the right road," she said. Sandy personally felt that the road was too close to town, but she turned and drove up the road anyway. She soon reached a house with two cars parked out front. "This doesn't look like a hideout," she said. "See, there's a house number and look - mail in the mailbox. This must be a private residence!" She carefully turned around and proceeded back to the highway.

The girls drove several more minutes without seeing any roads. Rose pointed out the turn-off to the trail head as Sandy drove past it. "Do you think we missed any side roads?" She asked. Sandy shook her head. "I'm inclined to believe that the gang's hideout would be past the trail head. The more isolated, the better." She spotted a small, rutted and nearly overgrown side road just as she said this. She pulled over and saw fresh tire tracks in the dirt road, which was the same reddish mud!

CHAPTER 24

Sandy parked her car at the side of the road. "I think we should follow this road on foot." Rose and Lily agreed, and the three were soon out of the car. Sandy locked the car doors and they began walking up the road. Sandy observed that there were many low hanging branches but the roadway was clear. Sandy observed tracks from several different vehicles, and guessed by how clear the tracks were that many of them were recent. She mentioned her suspicions to Rose and Lily, who agreed. Sandy suggested that they not talk anymore, since they didn't know how much further along the road the gang hideout might be. Rose and Lily agreed to this, too.

The three walked quietly along the rutted trail. Sandy kept her eyes open for any footprints alongside the roadway, but did not see any. "Perhaps the gang only drive in here," she mused. "I hope this road isn't miles and miles long!"

The girls continued walking in silence for nearly fifteen minutes, and then Sandy was gratified to see a small cabin up ahead. There were no cars parked out in front. She gestured to Rose and Lily, beckoning them over to the side of the road where they could conceal themselves among the trees. "Let's go around to the back of the cabin and see if we can find any indication of people here." The sisters agreed, and the three began to creep around the edge of the small clearing, keeping behind the trees.

Soon they reached the back door of the cabin. Lily peeped in a window, noting that the cabin appeared

to be all one room and sparsely furnished. "There's
no one in sight," she said, after she had come back
to where Rose and Sandy had concealed themselves.
"Let's go in and investigate!" she urged. Sandy was
torn - she wanted to look for any clues inside the
cabin, but she also did not want to lead the girls into
danger!

"Let's wait out here for ten minutes. We can all get
to positions where we can see into a window, and
if we don't see anyone inside, then after that time
we'll try the doors." She said she would take the back
window, Rose went around to the left of the house
and Lily went to the right. The girls crouched in the
trees and watched the inside of the cabin. Soon the
ten minutes passed, and Rose walked back to where
Sandy was waiting behind the back door.

"I'm sure there's no one inside. Let's get Lily and
go inside." Sandy agreed that there was no one hiding
inside the cabin. She and Rose walked over to the
right side of the house and told Lily that they were
going to go inside. Sandy led the way up to the back
door and tried the handle. It opened easily and,
breathing a sigh of relief that the door was not locked,
she led the girls inside. She saw that what Lily had
said was true: the cabin was very small and had one
large open room with a few cots against one wall, a
rudimentary kitchen and battered table and chairs in
another corner and only a few cupboards. Sandy saw
that the old stove was the wood burning type. There
was no oven or other appliances. In fact, there were
no light bulbs.

"I guess this place doesn't have electricity," Sandy
said, observing the candles and oil lantern set on the
table.

"I didn't see any lines running in," Lily added, "and I'm sure there wouldn't be underground lines run this far out into the country!" Sandy and Rose agreed. Fortunately, there was enough light coming in through the windows that the girls could see the room in detail. Sandy went first to the kitchen areas and began opening cabinets. She saw several stacks of canned food in one cupboard, and a box of paper plates and plastic cutlery in another. She noted that many of the disposable utensils were used up. She did not see a garbage can in the room, however. She looked at a can of green beans from the cupboard and saw that it was recently purchased.

"These cans don't expire for several years!" She called out, turning over several more to verify her hunch. "Someone's recently stocked these cupboards!" Rose came over to look, saying that she had found nothing of interest on the table. She agreed with Sandy that the cans were newly purchased. Sandy sorted through a few more, but found nothing else in the cupboard. She and Rose went over to where Lily was looking through the blankets and linens on the cots in the corner. Sandy noticed that there were four cots, all of which were made up. She saw that the blankets were low quality and a kind that could be purchased in any discount store throughout the country. "No clue there," she thought. Suddenly, Lily gave a cry. She held up a pair of shoes that she found underneath one of the cots, hidden by the dragging blanket.

Sandy took the shoes from Lily and looked them over. They were brown lace ups, of the type described by Betty. "These could be Peter Mullens' shoes!" she said, showing them to Rose. "If Betty recognizes these shoes, that will show without doubt that this was where the gang kept him!" Sandy turned the shoes over in her hands, looking for some other identifying mark but saw none. She looked under the other cots, even going so far as to pull the blankets off of them and look underneath the pillows. She saw nothing else of interest around any of the other cots. She told Lily what she and Rose found in the cupboards, and she also agreed that the food must have been purchased recently. She told the girls that she felt they should leave the cabin and report it to the police, who could send an officer to observe. "If this is the gang's hideout, they could return at any moment! We mustn't be caught here!"

She took the shoes Lily had found, saying that she would show them to the police and ask permission to show them to Betty at her house. The girls piled the blankets back on the cots close to the way they had been when they arrived and left by the back door. They walked back down the wooded road, keeping to the side in case a car should come down the road. They saw no one, though, and soon reached Sandy's car. Sandy quickly turned her car around and drove back through Valley Village and to Santa Maria. She pulled into the police station, and taking the shoes, went inside to speak with Officer Murray. He agreed to send an officer over to stake out the cabin, and took detailed notes on directions from Sandy. He said he would write a receipt for the shoes so Sandy could take them to show to Betty.

"Be sure to tell me whether or not she recognizes them," he said. Then he continued, "If that is the gang's hideout, which seems likely, I wonder where they went. We haven't been able to find out what color or make any of the other cars are, but it still seems foolish that they would take both vehicles out for the day. Perhaps they have a second hideout."

"That's very possible," Sandy said. "I would guess that they got nervous when they found out we have the white coupe. The red mud on the tires was a very good clue, and it's logical to assume that the police could find the cabin from the mud. The gang might have abandoned that hideout only recently and taken Peter Mullens to a secondary hideout." Officer Murray agreed, but said he felt they should still send an officer to stake out the cabin in case one of the gang members returned. He thanked Sandy for bringing the clues, and asked the girls to keep him updated on what Betty said about the shoes. Sandy promised she would, and the girls left.

She asked Rose and Lily if they would mind coming to her house to talk to Betty about the shoe and the sisters happily agreed. Sandy parked the car and the three walked inside. They found Mrs. Connors and Betty, holding baby Lisa, sitting on the couch in the living room, and looking very somber. "Mother, what's the matter?" Sandy asked, setting the shoes down. Mrs. Connors greeted her daughter and the Pinkerton sisters, then showed them a letter. "This was in the mailbox this afternoon. It's a ransom note for Peter Mullens!"

CHAPTER 25

"**A** ransom note!" Sandy gasped. Betty was holding Lisa on her lap, looking very upset. Sandy took the note and read it out loud. " 'Bring $100,000 in a bag to the bank in Valley Village by midnight tonight if you want to see your husband again. Do not call the police.' That's all the note says," Sandy looked at Rose and Lily, who also appeared shocked.

"What will I do, Sandy?" Betty asked. "I don't have that much money, but if I don't obey the note they'll kill Peter!" Betty's eyes began to well up and Sandy quickly crossed the room and put her arm around the woman. "Please, try not to worry. We will think of a way to outsmart them! Today, Rose and Lily and I found one of the gang's hideouts. We told the police and they've set up a watch on the cabin. Perhaps they will rescue your husband before the ransom is due!"

"But the note says not to tell the police. What if they find out and kill him?" Betty looked worried.

"I'm sure the police can help us, and the gang certainly has no way of finding out whether or not we tell them. I will phone the station this afternoon. Would you like to hear about what we found?" Sandy asked kindly, thinking it would distract Betty from her worry.

"Yes," Betty said. "Did you find any trace of my husband?"

"We did," Sandy said. She asked Rose to please bring in the shoes they found, and she handed them to Betty. "We found these underneath a cot in the cabin in the woods. The road to the cabin is a dirt road; the same red mud that was on the tires of the car. A group of three or four people has been hiding out in the cabin, though no one was there when we found it. We took these shoes - can you identify them as your husband's?"

"Let me see them," Betty said, taking the shoes from Sandy. She looked at them for several moments, turning them over in her hands. "Yes," she said after a minute, "these are Peter's shoes ... he was wearing these the night he went to meet those awful men! Now you say he's being held prisoner in a cabin in the middle of the woods and they want a huge ransom for him!" Betty began to cry. Mrs. Connors picked up Lisa and took her out of the room so the child wouldn't see her mother so upset.

"Please don't cry," Sandy said, "we will find your husband soon, I'm certain. With the help of Rose and Lily and the Santa Maria and Valley Village police, the gang can't hide much longer!" She handed Betty a handkerchief as Rose and Lily chimed in supporting Sandy's points. Soon Betty reached up and mopped her eyes with the handkerchief, thanking the girls for being so supportive. "I'm sure you're right, and it's terrible of me to be so doubtful after all the help you've already given me. I guess I lost my head for a moment. I'm quite sure it will all work out well now." She smiled at Sandy and the Pinkerton sisters, and then said she would go help Mrs. Connors prepare dinner. "Are you going to talk to the police now, or after dinner?"

"I think we should go now, if there's time before dinner is ready," Sandy said. "We can set up a plan with the officers for watching the cabin and perhaps surprising the gang tonight when they come to pick up the ransom." Rose and Lily agreed, and after

Sandy spoke with her mother and discovered dinner would not be ready for another hour, the three girls immediately left for the police station. Sandy took Peter Mullens' shoes with her to show Officer Murray, along with the ransom note. The girls arrived at the station and soon met with Officer Murray in the same conference room.

"Betty Mullens identified these shoes as the ones her husband, Peter, was wearing on the day he disappeared. I'm certain that the cabin where we found them is a hideout used by the gang." Officer Murray agreed. Sandy then showed him the ransom note. Officer Murray read the note, then looked up at the girls. His face was grim. "I don't like this," he said. "If the gang of men who've kidnapped Peter Mullens really is the same gang responsible for many Chicago area bank robberies, then he is in the hands of ruthless people. They've never yet killed anyone, but I believe they would be capable of it."

Sandy said she agreed it was a ruthless gang, but said the note puzzled her. "If the men wanted money, why didn't they demand it when Peter Mullens first went to meet them? Why wait so long to send a ransom note? Particularly because they must know that Betty Mullens doesn't have the money."

"Perhaps she does, though she may not know it," Officer Murray said. "If this is the gang I think it is, then they've made off with much more than $100,000 from all their robberies. If Peter Mullens was one of the gang, he would have a large sum of money from the robberies. Even though he left the gang years ago, he could have that money stashed away somewhere. Perhaps the gang thinks that his wife knows about the money and will give it to them to save her husband's life." Sandy agreed that did seem like a reasonable theory.

"I don't think Betty knows about any money though, if there even is any. She said she didn't have the money to pay the ransom, and I'm sure she was telling the truth. If her husband has a large sum of money hidden away anywhere, he's hidden it from her as well. What should she do about answering the demand?" Sandy asked. Officer Murray thought for a moment, and then replied.

"Usually, in cases like this, we leave a dummy sack full of paper at the requested drop-off locale. Several officers hide themselves around the area and watch and arrest anyone who comes for the dummy sack. Of course, in a situation like this where there's a group, that's running the risk that we might arrest a low level member of the gang and alert the man who runs the organization to be even more careful."

"And what if they don't receive the money and do kill Peter Mullens?" Lily asked.

"That is also something to consider," Officer Murray said. "Although, if the gang is convinced that he does have a large sum of money hidden away somewhere, they will be unlikely to harm him until they either have the money or know where it is. Given that they're making ransom demands of his wife, they clearly don't know where the money is right now. So I think we can assume that Mr. Mullens will be safe tonight, even if the gang does not get the ransom money. I think the best course of action would be to leave a dummy sack of fake money in the parking lot at the specified time." Sandy agreed with the that logic. She asked if he could set up a police watch on the parking lot to arrest anyone who came for the fake ransom.

"I will take care of that," Officer Murray said. "I also have an officer waiting outside the cabin in the woods to catch any member of the gang who goes back there tonight." Sandy thanked him, and then the girls got up to leave. "We will be in touch tomorrow to hear the results of the stakeouts," Sandy said. The girls got in her car to go home.

"Sandy," Rose spoke up suddenly, "that must have been what the doorbell and footprints were about! One of the gang members must have dropped off the ransom note in the mailbox this afternoon, rung the bell and then run away! Probably one of his shady friends was waiting in a car so he could make a quick escape."

"I'm sure that's what happened," Sandy agreed. "I wish I had gotten a look at the man, or at the car, however. Oh well." She sighed, then turned her thoughts to a more positive track and said, "Perhaps tonight the police will capture the gang and by tomorrow Peter Mullens will be safe!" She dropped Rose and Lily off at their house, promising to call in the morning as soon as she received any news about the results of the night's activities, and then drove to her own home, arriving just in time for dinner.

CHAPTER 26

Sandy sat down to dine with her family and Betty, who had put Lisa down for the evening prior to Sandy's arrival, and told her father about the ransom note. He was shocked by the brazen delivery method.

"I suppose it is reasonable that they would leave a ransom note for Betty."

"For Betty ..." Sandy suddenly jumped up from the table. "They know Betty's here! Oh, this could mean she's in great danger!" She excused herself, saying she must phone the police. Sandy quickly accomplished this, then returned to the dinner table, explaining that she had called the police station to request an officer be placed outside the Connors' house that evening to watch for anyone who made any attempt to enter and harm Betty or Lisa. "I can't believe none of us thought of that earlier!" she said, with a shake of her head. Her father commended her for the excellent clue, and then Sandy told him about what else she and the Pinkerton sisters had found that morning.

"I feel sure that the cabin in the woods is where the gang was hiding out. I hope they go back tonight and are captured!" she said, after explaining to her father about the clue of the red dirt and following it down the unpaved lane to the cabin. "We asked Mabel, the waitress in Valley Village, about hiking areas with red dirt on the ground near the town. She told us about a well known trail a few miles outside of town. The trail head was off of a very secluded and only lightly traveled rural highway just to the west of town. I thought there might be some cabins or shacks in that area the gang could use for a hideout. Rose and Lily and I followed her directions, only we took unpaved side roads to see where they led. A few miles past the road to the trail head we found the right one. The side road wound into the hills away from Valley Village far enough to be quite secluded. We saw the cabin, and inside were several cots, cans of food that were clearly newly purchased and a lantern. We found shoes that belong to Peter Mullens underneath one of the cots. We gave them to the police, in case there were any clues on them." Sandy's father asked what kind of clue they were hoping to find on the shoes. "There probably won't be anything," Sandy conceded, "But perhaps the police laboratory will find some other kind of soil or chemicals on the shoes that might tell us where else Peter Mullens has been since he was kidnapped."

Sandy then told the group about reporting all of the developments to the police, and the fake ransom trick. She hoped that some of the gang members would be caught when they came to get the sack. "The note said to leave the ransom in the parking lot of the Valley Village bank - the same bank where Peter Mullens was kidnapped, and the nearest bank to the cabin hideout in the mountains - so the police are going to leave the fake ransom there and stake out the parking lot. Anyone who touches the sack will be arrested." Mr. Connors said that was a smart plan, though perhaps the gang would see through it.

"If this really is a part of the Chicago bank robbery gang that has eluded the police for many years, then it is likely that they've encountered that ploy before," Mr. Connors said.

"That is true," Sandy said, "But I'm hoping that the gang will think Betty received the note, got scared and followed the instructions not to tell the police

and brought the money. We've figured that the gang
must think Peter Mullens has some large amount of
money stored away somewhere from his share of
the robberies years ago and they want to get that
back. They must be getting pretty desperate to be
kidnapping Peter Mullens so many years after he
escaped."

"I would imagine they've been searching for him
all these years," Mrs. Connors put it, "and only just
found him. If they believe he has money stored away,
it would be logical that they would attempt to get it
back after they kidnapped him. That's possibly also
what they wanted when they had planned to kidnap
Baby Lisa."

"Then what do you think they will do to my
husband after they find the money, if there even is any
money?" Betty asked, looking worried. "These people
were going to kidnap my child!" The Connors family
also looked worried. Sandy had to admit that there
was a high likelihood of Peter Mullens being hurt by
the gang if he were not rescued, or the money was
not provided to them soon. She emphasized that she
was sure the night watches by the police would bring
some results. Soon, the family finished dinner and
as Sandy helped clear the plates she hugged Betty.
"Please don't worry about your husband; the police
will surely catch some of the gang members tonight
and then there will be more clues about where to
search for him. I will do everything I can to find him
before he gets hurt!" Betty thanked the girl, then
after watching a short news program, she went up
to get ready for bed and check on her daughter. The
Connors family sat in the living room, listening to the
weather forecast for the next day.

"Sandy," Mr. Connors said, "what do you think is the real reason why Peter Mullens has become a target for this gang, so many years later?"

"I have to say I'm not sure," Sandy admitted. "That has been puzzling me, too. It's not logical that they should suddenly begin to seek him out. It is possible that certain members of the gang have been looking for him all these years and have just now found him and want the money he has. It also could be that the gang itself has either split into factions or even ceased to exist and other former gang members are seeking out people whom they believe to have stolen money stored away, from whom they can steal."

"That's a good idea," Mrs. Connors said. "If the gang has broken up, then many of the members might be unwilling or unable to earn a living in a legal way, so they're now trying to extort money to finance their lives from people they know and think have it."

The small family discussed several more ideas before deciding to turn the television set off and go to bed. Sandy and her father checked the locks on all the first floor doors and windows; Mrs. Connors checked the locks on the second floor windows and soon the family said good night and retired.

The next morning, Sandy was awake early, excited to hear the results of the police stakeouts. She went downstairs to prepare a nice breakfast for her father before he went to work. Sandy decided to make buttermilk pancakes and fruit salad and began to assemble the ingredients. Her mother and father had just come downstairs when the phone rang. Mrs. Connors answered it, and then said it was for

Sandy. Sandy was eager to take the call, so her mother took over cooking the food while she went to the phone.

"Hello, this is Sandy Connors," she said, expecting to hear the voice of Officer Murray on the other end of the line. Instead, she heard a gruff male voice say, "If you know what's good for you, you'll stop looking for Peter Mullens!"

CHAPTER 27

Sandy was shocked. "Who is this?" she asked, but the man who had spoken the warning had already hung up. She sat down in a chair near the telephone, deep in thought. It occurred to her that the man had not threatened Peter Mullens with any harm. "Perhaps the gang doesn't mean to harm him, they merely want any money he has hidden away," she thought. After a few more moments of thought, Sandy stood up and returned to the kitchen.

"Well, what did Officer Murray have to say?" her mother asked. "That was certainly a short report!"

"That wasn't Officer Murray on the phone," Sandy said as she helped her mother chop fruit to serve with the pancakes. Her father came into the kitchen as well, eager to hear what the report was. "It wasn't Officer Murray," Sandy repeated for her father's benefit. "That was a man who did not give his name, but he said I should stop looking for Peter Mullens." Sandy's parents looked grave.

"Did this man threaten you, Sandy?" her father asked.

"His exact words were 'If you know what's good for you, you'll stop looking for Peter Mullens.' There was no direct threat made against me, or anyone in the Mullens family. The man sounded very gruff, and he hung up immediately after delivering his message. I asked who he was, but the line was already dead." Sandy explained.

"Oh dear, I don't like this at all," Mrs. Connors said. "This sounds like it is becoming dangerous!"

"I feel that the gang is desperate," Sandy said.

"Leaving a ransom note on the chance that Betty Mullens knew where the money is seemed like a risky move, and the move of a gang that is no longer certain of their direction. Now, an anonymous threat seems even more desperate. The leader of the gang must be running out of ideas. I suppose this also shows that they discovered that the ransom money the police left was fake."

"And that not all the gang members were apprehended last night," Mr. Connors added. "The one who called you clearly is still at large." Sandy's mother agreed, cautioning her daughter to be careful. At that moment, the phone rang again. Mr. Connors stood up, saying he would answer it. He stepped into the hallway, and a moment later Sandy and her mother heard him saying "Good morning, Officer Murray. Hold on just one moment, please." Sandy went to take the call and was relieved to hear the police officer's voice on the other end of the line.

"Good morning, Officer Murray, What's the report?" Sandy asked.

"Unfortunately, there is very little good news to report. The men stationed at the bank did not see anyone approaching the fake ransom bag all evening; somehow the word must have gotten out. We took the bag back to the station after sunrise. I doubt any of the gang members would be coming to pick it up during daylight." Officer Murray explained.

"I agree the gang wouldn't show themselves during the day. Perhaps they came but saw the police officer waiting?" Sandy suggested.

"That's possible, though O'Malley has been a good officer for the station for nearly fifteen years. He knows very well how to keep hidden, so I'm more inclined to believe that somehow someone in the gang heard that the police had been notified and knew not to come pick up the ransom. If you think there's any hope of anyone coming looking for the money tomorrow, the same officer can go back to the parking lot with the bag tonight and wait again."

"No," Sandy said, "I don't think they would do that. How did the stakeout at the cabin in the woods turn out?"

"That also turned up nothing. Two officers - again, very experienced officers who know very well how to hide themselves and stay out of sight - waited outside the cabin all night. No one appeared. The men said they did not hear any cars slowing down or turning into the lane, either. The gang must have a second hide out, which they are using now. Perhaps they've abandoned the cabin in the woods permanently," Officer Murray suggested.

"That's unfortunate," Sandy said, disappointed, "now we'll have to begin looking for them all over again!"

"I've asked the same officers to stake out the cabin again tonight. While the gang surely does have another hideout, it's possible they alternate each night. If that's the case, they might be back to the cabin this evening and we will catch them. The fact that you found Peter Mullens' shoes in the cabin yesterday indicate that the gang has used it recently, so it seems worth the effort to stake it out a bit longer," Officer Murray said. "Do you have any ideas about where else the gang's hideout might be?"

"I have to admit I don't," Sandy said. "I thought the cabin was their only one - it's so close to the bank where Peter Mullens was kidnapped, and where they asked the ransom to be left. The other one must be near there as well. Rose and Lily and I will go out later today and see if we can find another abandoned cabin or similar location." Sandy then told the officer about the threatening phone call she had received that morning. "I wasn't able to find out anything about the man - he hung up as soon as he gave his message."

"What exactly did he say?" Officer Murray asked.

"The man said 'if you know what's good for you, you'll stop looking for Peter Mullens.' There was no direct threat to anyone - not myself, Peter, Betty or Lisa. I get the feeling that the gang is getting desperate. They did not get the money the wanted last night - whether they saw the officer or someone discovered that the police had been called in, or perhaps they realized that Betty Mullens didn't have the money they wanted. Now they're trying to scare me off the case because they know we're getting close to finding them," Sandy theorized.

"That's possible, Sandy," Officer Murray said. "Still, it's worrisome that they're threatening you. Even though there was no direct threat, it was implied by the call. You should be very cautious now when investigating anything - and I would recommend you always have one or more friend with you. Perhaps it would be safest for Mrs. Mullens and her daughter not to be alone, as well." Sandy thanked the officer for the advice and said she would heed it carefully.

"If there are any more developments, please let me know," she asked, then said goodbye. She returned to the kitchen and found that Betty Mullens had come downstairs while she was speaking to the police officer. She reported the negative results of both stakeouts, but emphasized that there were several possibilities still to investigate. She also told Betty about the threatening call and asked her to please be careful when leaving the house.

"In fact, if it's okay with you, it might be safer if you didn't leave the house. As much as it might be a bore, staying inside might be the best thing to keep you and Lisa safe," Sandy said.

"I agree with Sandy," Mrs. Connors said, adding that she would be home as much as possible and that everyone should take care to be sure that the front door was locked after every time anyone came inside the house.

"I also think we should all be careful to use the peephole to check on who's at the door every time the doorbell rings. At night, we should turn the porch light on as well, each time we open the door," Mr. Connors suggested. Everyone in the family agreed, and the four continued to discuss the case while they ate breakfast. Soon after, Mr. Connors left for work and Sandy went to call Rose and Lily, suggesting they come over and discuss the recent developments in the case. Within ten minutes, the Pinkerton sisters arrived and the three girls sat in the living room to talk about the report.

CHAPTER 28

Rose and Lily listened with rapt attention as Sandy brought them up to date on the recent occurrences. Both were shocked that none of the gang members were caught by either of the police stakeouts. "Somehow the gang must have discovered that the police were involved," Rose declared. "Otherwise, how would they have known not to go get the ransom in the parking lot?"

"I agree they were tipped off," Sandy said. "Of course, now there's the question of how they found out." Lily suggested that perhaps the girls had been spotted going into the police office and the leader of the gang had assumed that they were telling about the ransom note.

"That's a very good idea," Sandy said. "And unfortunately, the leader assumed correctly. Next time we will have to be much more careful. It didn't even occur to me to check to see if we were being followed when we went to the station!"

"Sandy," Rose began tentatively, "do you suppose we've been followed all this time? Perhaps that's also how the gang knew we had discovered the cabin in the woods." Sandy looked startled, then thought for a moment. "I'm sure we weren't followed that time," she declared. "I was watching carefully for any suspicious cars, and there was no one nearby. Perhaps we've only been followed a few times - maybe when we left from the house after the delivery of the ransom note!" Both sisters agreed that this was possibly what had happened.

"I would guess that once the gang found out we communicated with the police about the ransom note they thought we had told about the cabin in the woods, too, so they knew it wouldn't be safe to go back there," Lily said. Sandy and Rose agreed. Sandy next told the sisters about the threatening phone call she received that morning. Both were aghast.

"Sandy, this is becoming dangerous!" Lily said. "Do you think we should turn it over to the police and let them solve the rest of the case?"

"Of course we shouldn't!" Rose interjected, before Sandy had a chance to respond. "Betty and Lisa are depending on us to find Peter. We've found out much more than the police have, anyway!" Sandy said she agreed with Rose. "Besides, the man didn't actually directly threaten me with any harm," she said, "He just said I should stop looking for Peter Mullens." The young sleuth's face was set in an expression of determination. "Well, I'm not going to do that," she finished, "not when baby Lisa is depending on us to find her father!" Still looking a bit timid, Lily agreed that she also wanted to find Peter Mullens. Sandy sat back in her chair, her determined look fading into an expression of pensiveness.

"Now, however, I admit that I am stymied as to where to look next. I have a hunch that the gang is still in this area, still near the town of Valley Village, but I don't know of anywhere else they might be hiding and we have no clues to point us in the right direction." Rose and Lily also looked puzzled, and both admitted they did not know where else to look for the gang. Suddenly Rose jumped up from her seat.

"Lets go back to Valley Village!" She said. "Surely the gang buys groceries sometimes; we can get descriptions of some of the members from the police station and then go to the grocery stores and ask if they've been seen. Perhaps we'll get lucky and an employee in one of the stores will have overheard them talking about where they were going!"

"That's a good idea," Sandy said. "And we have no other clues to follow! Let's tell my mother and Betty where we're going, then stop by the station on our way out of town. We might get lucky and even be able to get a photograph of some of the gang from the police." Lily agreed to go along, and after Sandy had spoken with her mother briefly and told Betty where the three were headed, they drove to the station in Sandy's car. She was able to park quite near the door, and after looking around carefully to be sure there were no suspicious people lurking, the three went into the station.

Sandy spoke briefly with the receptionist, who said that Officer Murray was not on duty at that time, but she could page another office that was familiar with the case. Soon an older policeman came to speak to the girls. He introduced himself as Officer O'Malley. He said he had been assigned to wait at the Valley Village bank to apprehend anyone who came to pick up the ransom. "But not a soul showed up all night. The only person around was the night watchman, and he knew nothing about the ransom and did not try and tamper with the sack of fake money. In fact, I doubt he even saw it. We placed it in the far corner of the lot, under a tree, and the light was quite dim. But, how can I help you three?"

"Officer Murray mentioned that you had been assigned to that stakeout," Sandy said. "Thank you for your help." Rose and Lily also chimed in with thanks, which the Officer brushed aside, saying that it was his job to do stakeouts when his superiors asked him to. Sandy then went on to explain what the girls were planning that day. She briefly told about the dead end clue to the cabin in the woods, and said that they were now pursuing a hunch and wanted some information about the appearance of any of the gang members who had descriptions on file.

"We want to take this information to grocery stores in Valley Village and see if we can find a clerk or checker who recognizes any of the descriptions. Then we might be able to get some information about where the gang is now. If you have photographs of any of them on file, that would be even better," Sandy said. Officer O'Malley excused himself for a few moments, saying he would see what the station had on file. The girls sat in chairs situated close by to await his return. Sandy was deep in thought, wondering if this idea would bring about any more clues. She mentioned her concerns to Rose and Lily, saying, "I wonder, even if we do find a checker who recognizes one of the gang, whether we'll be able to get any information about where they're located now. Perhaps they don't discuss that in public!"

"That could be," Rose admitted, "but it was the only possible lead I could think of! Also, it seems to me that they've been getting sloppier recently. From what we've heard about how they used to operate, they would never have kidnapped someone and left a ransom note or allowed their hideout to be found so easily! Perhaps they've become sloppy in all they're doing."

"What if they've recently changed leaders, like Sandy suggested?" Lily interjected. "That would explain the change in activities, and the sloppiness."

"That's possible," Sandy said. "The former leader could be getting quite old by now if the gang has been in operation for nearly twenty years. Maybe the new leader isn't as experienced or doesn't have as much control over his men." The girls agreed that all these were possibilities. At that moment Officer O'Malley returned carrying a sheaf of papers. He gave these to Sandy, saying that these were all the descriptions the station had on file.

"Unfortunately, many of them are incomplete and lack names. It's even possible that some of these descriptions are of the same man. We have records of about fifteen sightings of gang members, stretching back across the last fifteen years. The most recent one is from five years ago." He pointed to several pictures that were near the back of the pile. "These are the only photos." Sandy took out the pictures, which showed two men walking near a large office building in a busy city. The pictures were fairly clear, despite having been taken from almost thirty feet away. Both men were middle aged, wearing sharply tailored suits and business shoes. Sandy saw that one of the men was carrying a briefcase.

"These men look just like legitimate business men!" She said, showing the photo to Rose and Lily.

"That's a theory about how the gang committed so many successful robberies - they all dressed and looked and acted very professional so the security personnel outside the bank did not become suspicious. Then they would ask for a private meeting with a banker and take money and negotiable securities from that private meeting so no one could step in to help. The men they stole from were threatened with dire punishments if they called the police." Officer O'Malley shook his head. "This gang is a bad lot, but led by a very intelligent man. They're one of the most successful gangs of bank robbers in history!"

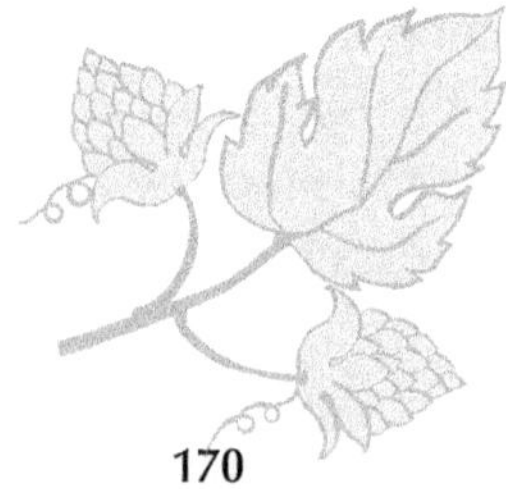

CHAPTER 29

Sandy was upset to hear how dangerous the gang was. After she and the Pinkerton sisters said goodbye to the officer, they went to Sandy's car, taking the photographs with them. Sandy also had notes from several of the descriptions of gang members that Officer O'Malley had shown the girls. She declared she would work even harder to find and rescue Peter Mullens now that she knew more about the danger he was in. Lily looked somewhat frightened about the prospect of meeting any one of the gang members, but Rose immediately declared that she would go with Sandy on all the attempts to find traces of Peter Mullens.

"We simply must find him before any harm comes to him; his daughter and wife are depending on us!" she said. Sandy agreed and Lily nodded hesitantly along with her. The three got into Sandy's car and the young sleuth began the drive to Valley Village. As she drove, she shared a more detailed plan with the sisters. "I think we should first stop at the restaurant we went to before, perhaps the waitress there has more information. We can certainly show her the photo Officer Murray gave us and see if she recognizes anyone. After that, I'd like to drive around to various local grocery stores and perhaps a few auto repair shops to see if any employees recognize anyone from the photos or descriptions. Hopefully someone we visit will have some information we can use to track down the gang's second hideout."

"Didn't you say that the police were going to stake out the cabin again tonight? Isn't it possible that they'll return there?" Lily asked.

"It is possible," Sandy conceded. "I personally feel that someone in the gang found out that the hideout had been discovered and they will continue to avoid it to keep safe. I'm glad the police are going to be watching it tonight, but I worry that nothing will come of it. We simply must find the gang's other hideout!" The three continued to discuss where the hideout might be as they drove toward Valley Village. Soon, Sandy turned the car onto the exit toward the town. She drove down the now familiar Main Street to the same restaurant. Sandy parked the car and the three alighted. "I hope Mabel is working this afternoon," Sandy said. She glanced at her watch and saw that it was nearly 1:30. "We're a little late for the lunch rush, she may have gone home."

To the young sleuth's delight, she saw that the friendly waitress was still at the restaurant. Shortly after the three were seated, Mabel approached the table. She recognized the girls after a few seconds and greeted them in a friendly manner. "What can I get you today?" She asked, order pad at the ready. Sandy and the girls ordered soup and sandwiches with iced tea, and then, as Mabel wrote down the luncheon requests, Sandy pulled the photographs out of her purse.

"Mabel, this might seem like an odd question, but have you ever seen either of these men before?" Sandy showed the pictures to the waitress after she finished notating the girls' orders.

"Well, I'm not rightly sure," Mabel said. "Seems to me there was a man that looked like this fellow here in the other day," Mabel pointed to a dark haired man on the left side of one of the photographs. "But he wasn't wearing any fancy suit. In fact, he was in pretty dirty workman's clothes. He looked like he hadn't showered in a few days. Could be the same man in this photo, though."

"Did he come in with anyone?" Sandy asked, excited that the waitress had recognized one of the men.

"Yes, there were three of them. They were all in dirty, torn up looking clothing. That one man is the only one that looks like anybody in this photograph, though. And come to think of it, he looks a lot older than this guy in this picture." Without revealing the reasons for her inquiries, Sandy continued to ask Mabel questions.

"What did these men talk about?" She asked.

"Well, I guess they worked together but they weren't very close. They hardly said a word to each other the whole time. They weren't very nice to me, either, just gave their order and didn't chat at all. The one who paid - the guy in this picture here - left a pretty stingy tip, too," Mabel huffed, clearly enjoying her role as the deliverer of prime gossip. "I don't know what they were in town for but I could guess they were working with that team of men who were doing the roof fixing down the street at the church. It was three days ago they were in; I haven't seen them since."

"Roofers? That sounds like it could be the man we're trying to find. How much longer is the roof work going on?" Sandy asked, feeling that the gang members certainly weren't working on roofs but perhaps tried to use that as a disguise.

"Well you're in luck," Mabel said. "The work is supposed to be finished by the end of the week. The crew is just right down Main Street a few blocks past the church on the left. You can't miss it!" Sandy thanked the woman for the information, and then Mabel went to put in the girls' lunch order.

"Surely you don't think a gang of former bank robbers that have kidnapped a local man have turned into mild mannered roofing professionals?" Lily asked, looking skeptical.

"No, I don't," Sandy said. "But I do believe that a gang of former bank robbers would be smart enough to take advantage of the presence of the group of roofers in town and try to make people believe they're here on legitimate business. It's too bad they didn't talk more freely while they were here," Sandy sighed.

"I guess they are professionals," Rose said. "They avoided police in Chicago for years so they certainly know how to keep their whereabouts a secret." Sandy agreed, saying that she had hoped Mabel's clue would provide a lead about where to look for the hideout.

"I guess we'll have to ask around other places in town," Lily said. "Like we originally planned." Sandy agreed. At that moment Mabel returned with the girls' orders, and the three ate heartily. The girls had just finished when Mabel returned to drop off the bill. Sandy, still seeking a helpful clue, stopped her and asked if she had happened to notice the vehicle the men drove to the restaurant. Mabel looked at Sandy in amusement. "I did happen to notice. I just was outside on a break when the men left. They hustled out to their car, didn't even wave goodbye! The man who paid drove away; it was a dark brown, old looking car. It didn't sound too good, either. The engine had a sort of a high-pitched wine whenever the car was moving. There was mud all over the tires and sides, too. In fact, the mud had splashed up so high that the headlights were entirely covered up. I guess those men don't drive too many places at night. I remember noticing the mud because it hadn't rained in a few days and the car was just covered in mud. Funny how some people don't take care of their cars." Mabel shook her head.

Sandy was excited by this clue, but she kept her face neutral as she left money to cover the bill and a generous tip. She and the sisters quietly left the restaurant after thanking Mabel for another delicious meal. Once the three had reached Sandy's car, she shared her excitement. "That sounds like the Mullens' car! And remember, girls, that car has also been missing since the night Peter went to meet with the gang. The white coupe was left in its place. I thought that the gang must have taken Peter Mullens' car and left one of theirs, this is proof that that's what happened." Sandy said that she still wanted to go to other establishments in town and ask for clues about the men, but she felt this clue was extremely valuable.

"If we don't find a clue in any other store nearby, we can follow the lead about the car to track the gang down!" She said eagerly.

CHAPTER 30

Sandy drove several blocks further down Main Street. She saw a sign indicating a local grocery store off to the left and pulled into the lot and parked her car. "Let's stay together for now, girls," she said. "Later, if we have several places to visit we can split up and go to them separately if we must, but since we have only one set of photographs I think it would be better to stay together as much as possible." Rose and Lily agreed, and the girls soon had entered the grocery store. Sandy saw that there were few customers inside the store at this hour and was glad they wouldn't have to delay a line of customers. Sandy saw a display of bottled drinks and selected one to purchase. Rose chose a pen from a rack near the counter and Lily also chose a bottled drink. Sandy took the meager purchases up to the check out and smiled at the clerk. The clerk, a middle-aged woman, smiled back.

"Hello, dear. You three are new in town, aren't you? I've worked here for twenty years and I know most everyone who lives around here," The woman, whose name tag identified her as Mona, began to ring up the items.

"Yes, we are from out of town," Sandy said. "I actually wanted to ask you something. Has this man ever been into this store?" Sandy showed the photograph to Mona.

"No, I don't think so," the clerk said, after squinting at the photo for several seconds. "He's sure all dressed fancy!"

"It's possible that at anytime when he visited this store he wouldn't have been in fancy clothes," Sandy said. She kept the photo in her hand where Mona could see it. "Are you certain you haven't ever seen him before?"

"No, ma'am. I know everyone who comes into this store, and this fellow hasn't been in before." With a sigh, Sandy thanked the clerk and paid, then took the items. She walked out of the store with Rose and Lily, who said, "Cheer up, detectives! We still have half a dozen places to go!" Sandy agreed, and then said that she hoped one of the shopkeepers could provide a clue. The three girls went next to a coffee shop on the corner, an ice cream parlor, a stationary store, a fruit and vegetable market and a liquor store. None of the clerks they spoke with had seen their quarry before.

"This is frustrating!" Rose said. "We know this man has been in this vicinity for a while now, but we can't seem to get a clue to where he's gone, and it's like he was never even here!"

"Maybe he's a survivalist type and lives off of his own land?" Lily suggested. Sandy suppressed a smile, knowing Lily was kidding, but nonetheless she reminded the sisters that the cabin had been stocked with canned food and there was no sign of any garden or farming activity near by. "Those cans were purchased somewhere!" She said.

"Perhaps he went to the store in disguise," Rose suggested.

"Or maybe someone else in the gang did the marketing," Lily added. Sandy agreed that those were both possible answers, but that those things would make finding the gang even harder. "We have only a picture of the leader; we don't really even know

what any of the other gang members look like. I think
we're going to have to come up with another plan."
The three girls were walking back towards Sandy's
car, discussing how else they might track down the
kidnappers, when suddenly Rose gasped. She pointed
towards an intersection in front of the girls and said,
"Isn't that the Mullens' car?" Lily and Sandy looked
closely at the brown coupe, which was idling at a red
light. Sandy saw that the driver of the car was a dark
haired man, heavy set, and wearing rough workman's
clothes.

"Quickly, girls," She called, running towards her
car, "Let's follow that car!" She jumped into her car,
started the engine and pulled out. Fortunately, her
car was parked in the same direction. She pulled into
the line of traffic with several cars between her car
and her quarry and asked the girls to keep their eyes
focused on the car ahead. "We'll follow him. If that
is one of the kidnappers, he may drive to the new
hideout!" The light turned green, and the line of traffic
began to move. Sandy was glad to see that, as the
cars moved down the road, several vehicles remained
between her car and the brown one.

"I hope he doesn't see us and try to shake us,"
she mused, still watching closely. To her surprise, the
brown car did not turn off of the Main Street until the
end, when he pulled onto the highway. "He's going
back toward Santa Maria!" Rose said, surprised.
"I wonder if the gang's new hideout isn't in Valley
Village?" Sandy said it was possible, but it was also
possible that the man was driving to another town, or
perhaps was going somewhere other than the hideout.

"I don't think he suspects that he's being followed.
He's driving slowly and not trying to lose us," Lily

pointed out. Sandy agreed, and said that she hoped it would stay that way. The brown car was proceeding at a pace several miles below the posted speed limit, so Sandy also drove slowly. She dropped back even further and let several more cars pull in between her vehicle and the one she was following. "Girls, please do keep your eyes out for any turns he makes. I don't want to lose him, but I also want to be sure we aren't spotted." The two sisters kept their eyes open and closely watched the brown coupe, but the car did not turn off of the highway until he had reached Santa Maria. Sandy pulled off at the same exit, and followed the car through the series of turns, being careful to remain a good distance back.

"Sandy," Rose began, after the two cars had proceeded some distance from the highway, "aren't we nearing your house?"

"We are," Sandy said grimly. "I wonder if that's where this man is going." When she saw the car turn into the entrance to her neighborhood, she pulled her car over to the side of the road. "Lily, please take the car keys and wait here. He's driving slowly on these neighborhood streets; I should be able to keep him in sight. I'm going to see where he goes!" She quickly got out of the car and walked down the sidewalk, keeping her face in the shadow of the trees. With a sinking heart, she saw that the brown car had pulled over to the roadside just across from her house. The driver was sitting inside, and seemed to be watching the Connors' house. Sandy stopped walking. She thought for a few moments, and then quickly retraced her steps to her own car.

"Lily, Rose, the man is watching my house. I'm going to sneak around and into the back yard and phone the police. Please stay here with my car, and if he comes out this way follow him. I will have the police drive in from the other side of the street so he won't be able to get away." Sandy thanked the girls for their help, then dashed around the block the other way and went into her house. She outlined the situation to her mother and Betty, asking them not to look out the windows, then immediately called the station. Quickly telling the story to the officer who answered, she asked that a police car be sent. "Please leave the sirens off until you reach the street and see the car. If he hears sirens he will drive off and my friends may lose him." The officer promised it would be done, and said a squad car was on the way. Sandy asked that Officer Murray be notified of the new developments, saying he was working on the case. The man promised to send the officer to the Connors' house right away.

Sandy hung up and went toward the front door. She resisted the urge to peek outside, waiting instead to hear the sounds of the approaching police car. Soon she did hear a car engine, then the sounds of a car starting. "I guess the driver of the brown car is trying to get away," Sandy noted, hearing squealing tires. The engines of both cars roared, then Sandy was shocked to hear a large crash - the screech of metal and tinkling of glass, then quiet as both car engines stopped!

CHAPTER 31

Aghast, Sandy ran to the window and peeked out through the blinds, which she had asked her mother to lower. She saw the brown coupe and a police car smashed together in the middle of the road. It appeared that the cars had collided head on. Sandy was concerned; she did not see anyone standing outside the wreckage. "I hope they aren't trapped inside!" she thought. She asked her mother to phone the police and tell them about the accident, and she ran outside to see if she could help either of the drivers. "Even if the man in the brown coupe did kidnap Peter Mullens, he doesn't deserve to die in a car crash!"

Sandy quickly reached the mangled cars, and peeking inside was shocked to see that neither vehicle had an occupant! She looked around the pavement, to see if either man had been thrown out of the car by the force of the collision, but she saw no one nearby. At that moment, the neighbor's door opened and a young woman came running down the drive. She reached Sandy and introduced herself as Melanie Potter, saying she was a health care aid for Sandy's elderly neighbor, Mrs. Johnson.

"I saw the crash," Melanie said. "I've phoned the police and another officer is on the way. You aren't hurt?"

"No," Sandy said, unsure of how much about the crash she should tell Melanie. "I heard the collision from inside my house. I've asked my mother to phone the police as well. I came down to see if I could help anyone, but these cars are both empty!" She was mystified as to where the drivers had gone.

"The drivers both jumped out before the crash," Melanie said. "I saw the whole thing. The brown car was parked here, and when the police car came around the corner, the man in the car quickly started the engine and drove very fast, directly at the police car. The policeman tried to swerve out of the way but the driver kept going straight at him. Just before the cars were going to hit, the man in the brown car opened the door and jumped out. The policeman did the same, though how he managed to get out in time, I'm not sure. I know they both got away because right after the cars hit, I saw the driver of the brown car running towards the main road, with the policeman chasing him."

"I see," Sandy said, inwardly glad that neither man had been hurt and hoping that the policeman would catch the criminal. "Thank you for explaining - I've been looking for bodies of people that were thrown clear, but now I know no one was hurt!" She smiled at Melanie, thinking joyfully that if the driver of the brown car ran toward the road, Rose and Lily should have been able to help the police officer apprehend him. She told Melanie that she would wait by the crash until the other police officer arrived and explain what happened.

"The officers might want to speak with you since you are the only witness to the crash, but until then I'm sure it will be alright for you to return to Mrs. Johnson's house," Sandy said. Melanie thanked Sandy, saying she would be glad to speak with the police once they arrived. "I worry about leaving Mrs. Johnson alone, though. She's quite forgetful and has fallen several times recently and can't usually get up without help." With a friendly wave, the health care aid returned to her patient's house, and Sandy continued to look over the sight of the crash. She saw that the cars, though damaged at the front ends, did not appear to be beyond repair.

"I wonder if there are any clues in the back of the coupe," she thought. Sandy knew it would be illegal to remove anything from the car until after the police had come, photographed the scene and taken notes on what had occurred. She could not resist the temptation to look inside the back seat of the car and see what was there. To her delight, she saw several file folders and many scraps of paper scattered about. She surmised that in the crash, the folders had been flung forward from the seat and the papers had fallen out. Sandy was unable to read any of the papers, but she could see that all the folders were labeled. "I hope that the crash did not mix up the papers so we won't be able to put the correct papers back in the correct files! The proper labels could tell us much about what these papers mean!" She thought.

At that moment, she heard sirens and a second police car pulled into the road. Sandy was pleased to see Officer Murray, who parked near the crash and was soon speaking to her. She explained how the crash came about, saying she thought the driver might attempt to flee but she hadn't imagined he would cause such a dangerous accident. She told the officer what Melanie had seen and pointed to the house where the young woman was staying. Officer Murray noted her name and address and said he would speak with her after he looked over the crash site.

"The officer in this car jumped out and ran off chasing a suspect, you say?" Officer Murray looked pensive. "If that's the case, hopefully we will hear soon that he has caught his man and will return. Neither of the men could be running very fast or very far after bailing out of a crash like this. Even though the street is short, it looks like the brown coupe was traveling quite fast when they collided. Jumping out of that car must have been a pretty desperate move!" The officer now pulled a camera out of his car, saying he would take pictures of the scene. He took several, including one of the skid marks on either side of the crash and the broken glass and twisted metal that had fallen off of the wreckage.

Sandy stood off to the side of the broken vehicles, wondering why the driver of the brown car had decided to cause the accident. "The gang is desperate. The demand for ransom didn't work, and so now they're making riskier moves, like staking out my house and causing an accident when the police show up. I hope the officer chasing him catches his criminal!" she thought to herself, also hoping that the police officer was uninjured. At that moment, Officer Murray declared he was finished taking photos and was going to radio a report back to headquarters. Sandy said she wanted to see if Rose and Lily were all right, and would tell them about the crash. She walked the few blocks to her car and, seeing the sisters still waiting there, informed them about the crash.

Both were shocked. Rose said that no policeman had run past, adding that possibly the suspect had turned off the main road before reaching them. Sandy agreed that was possible and said she felt there was no use in the girls staying there any longer. She got into her car and drove the three the few blocks back to her house. She pulled the car into her garage, noting that the policeman still had not returned. The three girls again walked down to the site of the crash, which now had several curious neighbors surrounding it. Officer Murray was explaining that no one was injured and asked the bystanders to stay back.

Sandy now asked the man if there was any way she would be allowed to remove the documents from the back seat of the brown car and examine them. Officer Murray said that unfortunately, nothing could be removed from the site of the crash. "These cars will be towed to the station and then anything remaining in the vehicles will be removed. If you would like, I will have you called in to examine whatever is found inside this brown car, after our examination of it has been finished." Sandy thanked the him, saying she could see papers lying in the backseat and she hoped they might furnish a clue about where the gang was now hiding with Peter Mullens.

Suddenly, Rose gasped. She pointed to a yard on the side of a nearby house, from which the girls could see the police officer returning. Sandy was thrilled to see he was leading the driver of the brown car back in handcuffs and both men appeared unhurt.

CHAPTER 32

Sandy called to Lily, and the three girls immediately rushed over to the policemen, hoping to hear the prisoner's story. Officer Murray still had his pad of notepaper out and he began to take notes. The man was breathing heavily, apparently from the chase through the neighborhood, and told his story in small snatches. The man had gotten no further than telling that he came to the neighborhood to spy on Sandy when it became apparent that the running chase had overtaxed the man. Officer Murray said the prisoner would have to be taken to a hospital.

"Sandy, once this man has been treated, we will formally arrest him and take down in writing any confession he gives us. We will have you come to the station to hear the confession," the officer said. Sandy thanked Officer Murray, who said he would radio for another squad car to come and pick up the first officer. A police tow truck was already on the way. He then departed with the prisoner in his car, heading towards Santa Maria hospital. Sandy turned to the first officer, hoping he could tell something about the chase.

"Would you like to come inside and rest?" She asked him, aware that the chase had been arduous. The policeman insisted that he was feeling fine, adding that the prisoner was much older than he and seemed to be in poor physical condition. "Besides, I should stay by these wrecks until the towing crew and back-up arrive."

"May I ask you what happened?" Sandy asked. "I heard the crash from my house but did not see it. And what exactly happened when you were chasing the man?"

"Well, I received a call to come here and apprehend a suspect who was in a vehicle," the young policeman, who identified himself as Wicks, began. "Usually, when there's a suspect in a car, he stays in the car. Sometimes there's a chase in the vehicles. I came prepared for the driver to turn suddenly or attempt to dart around me and drive off in the other direction, but as soon as I turned onto this street, the man drove straight at me. I swerved right and left to shake him, but he stayed directly in front of me. He seemed to be going fast, though given how short the street is it probably wasn't in excess of thirty miles per hour. Right before the cars were going to crash, I put on my brakes. The suspect jumped out of his car, rolled away and made as if to run off. Well, I could tell that there was no way I would be able to avoid a crash so I jumped out, too. I was on the other side of the road and saw the suspect running into the woods. My vehicle had been going much slower when I jumped out so I was uninjured. I got up and chased after the man. We ran down the street, then he turned into a yard and ran through to another street, turned onto it and was just making a turn again into a yard when I caught up with him. He seemed to be favoring his left leg; that slowed him down toward the end of the chase. For an older man who had just jumped out of a car he was running pretty fast!"

"Perhaps that was the adrenaline," Sandy put in as Wicks paused in his story.

"Likely it was," the policeman agreed. "Whatever the reason, it slowed him down enough that I was able to catch him. So I put cuffs on him, placed him under arrest and brought him back here. I guess you saw the rest. Officer Murray was worried about the suspect's health because he was still wheezing and panting, so he took him to the hospital and I guess he will be charged there. Why was he staking out your house?" Wicks asked, looking curiously at the young detective. Sandy told a brief version of the mystery thus far, adding that the wife of the kidnapped man and his young child were staying with her. "I called the police because I feared for their safety, and I hoped that arresting one of the leaders of the kidnapping gang would mean we could find and rescue Peter Mullens. Did the man say anything to you while you were running, or as you brought him back here?"

"He didn't say a word. Though he was panting so hard he couldn't speak and while we were running he was focused on getting away, not talking," Wicks said. At that moment, the tow truck and other police officers arrived. Sandy thanked Wicks for telling her about the crash and then she and the Pinkertons returned to Sandy's house to get out of the way of the towing crew. Sandy found her mother and Betty inside, peeking out the window. She told the two women what had happened, adding that she expected a call from Officer Murray later that afternoon or the next day with information about a confession from the driver of the brown car. Betty said that the brown coupe was the car Peter had taken to meet the man at the bank the previous week, adding that it had belonged to the friend who was sheltering them and had recently passed away. "I guess your theory about the gang taking that car and leaving one of their own in its place was correct, Sandy," she said. Betty then excused herself, saying that she needed to go prepare lunch for Lisa, who was in her crib upstairs.

Sandy, Rose, Lily and Mrs. Connors prepared a light lunch of soup and a salad and discussed the mystery while they ate. Sandy said she hoped that the arrested man would soon confess and tell where Peter Mullens was being held. "He looked like the man in the photograph thought to have been the leader of the gang. Perhaps without his leadership the gang will fall apart and Peter will be released!" Lily said.

"That would be nice, but I'm worried that the gang is too desperate for that. They know they've been found out and are wanted for kidnapping. It's unlikely that they would let Peter go without getting the reward they were seeking, though so far there's been no evidence presented that shows there even is a pile of money anywhere!" Mrs. Connors shared her opinion.

"What if there isn't any money?" Rose asked. "Betty doesn't know anything about any reward, and I find it highly unlikely that her husband would have spent so many years with her and not told her about the money. What if Peter Mullens had been killed in some accident? That would mean that his wife and daughter would have been deprived of the money. I can't imagine that a good husband and father, like Peter Mullens appears to be, would take that risk."

"I'm inclined to agree, Rose," Sandy said. "Of course, Peter did tell his wife that there were things from his past that he didn't share, so perhaps he kept the money secret too because it was related to his previous criminal activities." Mrs. Connors said she felt sure that the gang was just becoming desperate and grasping at straws, and that there was no such money hidden anywhere. "Some people just won't do honest work!" she said, shaking her head. Soon the group had finished lunch and moved into Sandy's living room. Sandy looked out the window and saw that the crashed automobiles had been removed and the street swept. "It almost looks like nothing happened here!" she thought. "I do hope that the crash leaves behind a clue!"

CHAPTER 33

Sandy and the other girls discussed the mystery throughout the afternoon. Sandy eagerly awaited news from Officer Murray about the suspect's confession. She was not disappointed, as the policeman called shortly before 5 o'clock, saying that the suspect had given the police a fair amount of information regarding the prior bank robberies and the kidnapping. "Why don't you come over to the station with the rest of your detective team and read the confession. The hospital is keeping the man overnight - I gather he has heart problems and they want to observe him and make sure no serious health issues arise." Sandy thanked the officer and said she would come to the station shortly with Rose and Lily.

Sandy informed her mother about the officer's call, saying she would be back as soon as she could. Mrs. Connors planned a late dinner since Sandy's father had an after work meeting, so the family wouldn't be eating until 8 PM. As the three girls drove to the station, Sandy told the Pinkerton sisters about the suspect's confession and his overnight hospital stay, adding that she hoped the suspect would be able to answer some questions the next day. Soon the three reached the police station and were immediately shown inside to the meeting room. Officer Murray was waiting with a copy of the written confession, which was quite long. After the girls had taken seats, he explained.

"The suspect, whose name is Jonas Becker, gave a complete confession, beginning with the bank robberies in Chicago dating back nearly twenty years.

Apparently Becker's father, who is now deceased, was the original leader of the gang. Becker and several other children of members of the gang joined as they grew up, and Becker took over the leadership ten years ago, after Peter Mullens had left," Officer Murray said.

"So that means that the photograph we had of the gang members - including one that we thought was Becker - was actually taken before Becker joined the gang?" Sandy asked, remembering that date given to accompany the picture.

"That is correct," Officer Murray said. "Jonas Becker - the man we have in custody - looks quite similar to his deceased father, Clarence Becker. Clarence Becker is the man in the photograph."

"What an amazing coincidence that they should look so alike!" Sandy said, recalling that several people in Valley Village had recognized Jonas Becker as the man in the photograph when it was really his father. Officer Murray agreed, and then continued with the narration of the confession.

"I will skip over some of the things he mentioned that pertain only to the robberies, with your permission. Becker said that a young man, whom we know as Peter Mullens, but was then known as Peter Simpson, joined the gang several years after Becker. Simpson was apparently a crack safe breaker, but he wanted out after a few years when the gang became more aggressive. Simpson disappeared one day, around a time when two other gang members had also disappeared - Charles and Parker Kent, two brothers who worked with Simpson breaking safes. At this time, the gang also discovered that nearly $200,000 had been taken from the accounts. They had several accounts under pseudonyms at banks all over the Chicago area. Becker - Clarence Becker, that is - was the only person who had access to them all. It was assumed that the Kents and Simpson had left together, taking with them the $200,000.

"The gang was doing very well, though, and did not miss the money immediately. However, following Clarence Becker's death, the leadership began to fall apart. Jonas Becker took over, but apparently did not have his father's logical mind and several robberies failed. Some gang members were caught, and the last confirmed robbery by this gang occurred five years ago. It was assumed that the gang had disbanded to avoid arrest. None of the money taken in any of the robberies was ever found. According to Becker, most of the gang did disband following the unsuccessful robberies. However, four of the members stayed together: Becker himself, Frank Robbins, Toby Sampson and Marlon Hawkins. These four men had access to the money remaining from the gang's hauls. I gather they paid off the members who left with a paltry sum, saying that there was much less money remaining than there really was, and helped themselves to the rest. They left Chicago and went down to Florida where, Becker swears, they did not commit any more robberies. Then, about six months ago, Becker saw in the newspaper an obituary for Charles Kent that stated that the man had died impecunious in a state mental facility, leaving no descendants. The obituary added that Charles' brother Parker had died in prison two years earlier. What Parker Kent was arrested for is unclear, as is why Charles Kent wound up in a mental facility. But the obituary did tell Becker that the Kents did not have the $200,000. He assumed that Simpson had taken it with him.

"Now, Peter Simpson, or Mullens now, his side of the story is not yet known. But Becker said that he scoured the country for men named Peter who matched the description of Peter Simpson. He claims he called in favors from several criminal acquaintances, one of who told about making a fake ID for a man named Peter Simpson (the new name of the fake ID was Peter Mullens) at the same time as Simpson had taken off from Chicago. Becker was able to find Peter Mullens by looking up car registrations, house liens, bank account information and other things that he was able to access by calling upon other old criminal friends. He traced Mullens to Chicago, and then followed him after Mullens left Chicago attempting to get away. Becker found out he had a wife and a daughter and began to blackmail him in hopes of getting the remaining money that he was sure Mullens had.

"Becker sent messages to Mullens via the newspaper classifieds section, using a code which the gang used years before. Becker says that Mullens at first denied all knowledge of the gang and any money, but after Becker threatened his wife and children, they met one night at the Valley Village bank, last week. Becker and his three friends were there, and they kidnapped Mullens. Becker then sent the ransom note to Mullens' wife because he was sure that she would know where the money was hidden. He had someone watching your house this whole time, Sandy, and when the watcher spotted you going to the police after the ransom note was sent, Becker called off the operation to retrieve the ransom because he was sure that the bank was being watched.

"Also, a sharp-eyed cohort of Becker's saw the tire tracks in the dirt road and recognized them as different than the tracks from the gang's cars after you three found their cabin hideout and that's why they didn't return. Becker said that the gang gave Peter Mullens some spare clothes, including several other pairs of shoes, so the shoes the three of you discovered inside the cabin weren't missed by anyone. The gang is using a new hideout now - an abandoned warehouse outside of Santa Maria - and the remaining three criminals as well as Peter Mullens are there now. Becker swears that Mullens has not been mistreated in anyway and would have been immediately released after the gang received the ransom money. We have directions to the warehouse; we're going to send a rescue team out this evening."

"That's wonderful!" Sandy said, as Rose and Lily began to clap. Officer Murray said that the police would bring all the gang members and Peter Mullens back to the Santa Maria police station following the arrest. "Becker did admit that the gang is armed, so it wouldn't be safe for any of you, or Mrs. Mullens, to accompany the police on the rescue mission. We are certain that we can rescue Peter Mullens safely, however, and we should be back to the station by ten o'clock, if you want to come back then."

CHAPTER 34

Sandy and the Pinkerton sisters felt like cheering; all three were certain that Peter Mullens would be back safely by that evening. Sandy thanked Officer Murray for calling them in and allowing them to hear Becker's confession. The three then left, eager to share the good news with Betty. "Girls, why don't you come back to my house with me. You can call your parents as soon as we get home and stay for dinner. I'm sure Mom cooked enough. Then, when we hear from the police that Peter Mullens has been rescued we will all three be ready to go down to the station immediately. Betty and Lisa will come with us, too." Rose and Lily agreed that was a sensible plan, and as soon as the three returned to the Connors' house, Lily placed a call to her parents and within an hour the two girls, the Connors family and Betty and Lisa Mullens sat down to dinner.

"Well, Sandy, I hear there has been some excitement today!" Mr. Connors began, after everyone was seated and he said grace. "Something about a car crash, a captured criminal and a confession!"

"That is about how it happened," Sandy said with a laugh. She explained the girls' activities of that day to her father, starting with the unsuccessful trip to Valley Village to search for the second hiding place of the gang. "I guess it wasn't completely unsuccessful - in a roundabout way, it did lead us to their second hideout, but there was a car crash and a police chase first!"

"Imagine that!" Betty interjected. "I had no idea the former associates of my husband were so dangerous!"

"Don't feel badly, my dear," Mrs. Connors said. "From what this Becker fellow explained in his confession, it sounds like the gang wasn't so bad at first and then your husband left as soon as he could after the group became violent."

"That's true," Sandy said. "And extreme poverty can put people in desperate situations. Peter likely thought that he wouldn't be able to find food for himself without turning to a life of crime."

"I guess so," Betty said, looking at her daughter. "I'm glad Lisa will never experience that. Peter and I have taken legal steps so that even if we should both be in a accident, she will be protected." Everyone agreed that was a prudent plan, and then the discussion turned to speculation about how the police raid on the hideout was proceeding. "I hope no one is injured for my family's sake," Betty said, looking worried. "Officer Murray didn't want any of us to go on the raid with the officers because he worried the remaining gang members might be armed!"

"That is possible," Sandy said, but added that police officers received extensive training about what to do in situations where they faced armed criminals. "I'm sure the men Officer Murray is bringing along on the rescue mission are all well trained and know how to react and respond in that case."

"The police of Santa Maria are especially well trained, actually," Rose said. "Dad works for the court system and he's seen some cases from neighboring towns where police departments were sued because the officers didn't know how to react in hostage and other dangerous situations. He said he's looked at the training requirements from these towns compared to those in Santa Maria and that the police here receive much more extensive and detailed training and have many more hours to complete." Sandy could see that Betty looked comforted by this information and she smiled at Rose to thank her for helping ease the woman's fears.

The small group presently finished dinner and Mrs. Connors brought out a special cake she had baked to celebrate the capture of the criminal. She had frosted and hidden it away while Sandy and the Pinkertons were at the police station and the three girls were greatly surprised and pleased to have the special treat. The group laughed and joked merrily while they ate, and everyone was gratified to see that Betty no longer appeared worried and seemed excited that her husband would soon be free and returned to her and their young daughter. After the cake was consumed, Betty excused herself to take Lisa upstairs for her bath. The three young people cleared the table and soon the dishes were washed and put away.

Everyone retired to the living room to watch the news broadcast, but Sandy was far too excited by the imminent news of the mystery's completion to pay attention to the broadcast. She paced about the room and checked the clock every few minutes, hoping that ten o'clock would arrive. She was startled to hear Rose gasp and call her name at quarter to ten, gesturing to the TV and telling Sandy she must hear the featured story. Sandy took a seat in a chair close to the television set where she could hear the broadcaster clearly and was startled by what she heard. The entire group sat listening to the news story about a police chase down the highway near Santa Maria that was currently in progress.

"We will be bringing you news updates as we hear more," the broadcaster stated, adding that it was not known who the police were chasing or why. "Do you suppose that could be the rest of the gang? Were they able to rescue Peter Mullens?" Mrs. Connors wondered out loud. Sandy was silent, but she watched the broadcast, hoping for another update.

"I suppose if you hear from Officer Murray before the chase concludes then you can assume it's another criminal involved in the chase on TV," Mr. Connors said.

"It is near ten now," Lily said. "If the chase doesn't involve the gang Officer Murray is out to catch, we should be hearing any minute now." Sandy agreed that would be a good indicator, and the group remained seated, listening intently for the ringing of the telephone or an update on the chase occurring on the highway.

Ten o'clock came and there was no phone call. The clocks struck quarter past ten and still Officer Murray had not called. Sandy had just made up her mind that the chase broadcast on the news must still be ongoing and somehow involved the criminals she hoped to hear were captured that evening, when the broadcaster announced a special bulletin, saying that the police chase mentioned earlier that evening had been successfully resolved. "We have received news that three criminals who attempted to flee arrest from a warehouse outside of the city have been arrested after a chase lasting some twenty minutes and covering a variety of local roads. A man who was held hostage by the criminals has been rescued and there have been no injuries reported. We repeat, the chase

is ended, the criminals have been arrested and no one
has been hurt."

Everyone in the room cheered. Sandy was
sure now that the featured chase was, in fact, the
remaining members of the gang of kidnappers and
bank robbers. And now they had been caught, and
the hostage was rescued and uninjured! Sandy shared
her thoughts with the others in the room, who agreed.
The five continued to watch the broadcast, hoping
that another update would be provided, but another
quarter of an hour passed without word. At that
moment, the telephone rang. Sandy was sure it was
Officer Murray.

"Hello?" She said.

"Sandy," Officer Murray sounded tired but happy.
"The rescue was successful. The criminals almost got
away - once you arrive at the station I will tell you
the whole story - but Peter Mullens is here, safe and
sound. He would like to see his wife and daughter.
Can the five of you come to the station right away?"
Sandy said she would immediately tell the other girls
and the group would be at the station within ten
minutes.

CHAPTER 35

Sandy told Rose, Lily and Betty about the results of the chase and the four were soon heading towards the station with Lisa in Betty's arms. Despite the somewhat harried departure from the Connors household, Lisa was sleeping peacefully.

"The poor dear. She's missed her father," Betty said as the car sped along as fast as the speed limit allowed. "She's too young to understand why he's gone or how long it's been but I tried to explain to her that he didn't leave on purpose. She will be glad to see him again!" Sandy smiled at the young girl, and soon the four women and the baby arrived at the police station.

There were few cars in the lot at this hour. Sandy surmised that her car was the only one carrying visitors, and parked in a spot as close to the front door as possible. The girls got out of the car and locked the doors before going into the station. The young receptionist at the counter greeted the small group and immediately directed them into a room. Betty, very excited now to see her husband, walked ahead of the group and into the room first. The girls heard her exclamation of delight, followed by an excited greeting in a male voice and lingered in the hallway for several moments.

Soon, however, Sandy and the Pinkerton sisters entered the room. Betty was standing beside a tall man with light brown hair and pale skin. Sandy thought perhaps he looked a tad paler than was healthy, but presumed it was due to the stresses of his past week. Betty introduced him as her husband,

Peter Mullens. The girls all shook the man's hand and Peter thanked Sandy profusely for helping bring about his rescue. Officer Murray, who had been standing in a corner of the room, now came forward and suggested that the group sit down and share their stories with each other. He asked Sandy to first share what had happened since Peter Mullens' capture so he would know the situation.

Sandy obliged, and told the man of events following Betty's arrival on her doorstep the day after his disappearance. The man looked surprised and angry at some points, and gasped when he heard that the brown car belonging to his friend had been totaled. Sandy reminded the group that the papers in the back of the car had yet to be examined. "What significance do you think they could have, now that we've captured the criminals and solved the case?" Rose wondered.

"We still have a few pieces of the puzzle left to solve, but they can wait until tomorrow," Sandy said. She finished telling about the capture of Jonas Becker and his confession. Officer Murray added that Becker was in custody, though he was still under doctor's watch at the hospital to monitor his heart, which was still very weak. The police officer then began to tell about the car chase and final capture of the remaining criminals. "We knew where the warehouse was from Becker's testimony. He also said there were weapons out there, though he said usually the men did not carry them when they were in their hideout. Well, we went out with a group of ten officers and I guess because the gang had expected Becker to return somewhat earlier, they were suspicious. They were all armed and began to fire when they heard multiple cars approaching. They got in several lucky shots and disabled three of the five vehicles we took to the scene. I ordered my men not to return fire because we were afraid of hitting Mr. Mullens. Some minutes later - presuming, I suppose, that we had been killed or injured because no one was firing back - the gang left out the back door to a hidden car and tried to drive away. They had Mr. Mullens with his hands tied together and put him in the back of the car.

"Well, once we saw that they were getting into a car, four officers took the two remaining vehicles and gave chase, which went through several surface streets and onto a rural highway, but in the end we were able to catch them when their vehicle ran out of gas about fifteen miles away. We took them into custody, released Mr. Mullens' hands and returned to Santa Maria. The chase and shoot out took longer than we had expected, so we were somewhat later in our return than planned, as I'm sure you noticed." Officer Murray grinned as he finished his recitation. Sandy told the officer what the girls had heard on the television news broadcast. "We figured that the chase involved Mr. Mullens and the bank robber gang when mention was made of a warehouse and a hostage. But the newscast did tell us that everyone was safe and the criminals had been captured, so we weren't too worried. One question, though, how did the officers whose cars had been disabled get back into town?"

"We called for back-up, but the chase began before it arrived. Once we had the fugitives in custody we picked up the stranded officers and the secondary team. Tow trucks will bring the cars back tomorrow, and our mechanics will fix up the tires and any other damage," the officer explained. He then turned to Peter Mullens and asked the man to tell his side of the story, beginning from his capture. Murray suggested that the Mullens could tell the whole story to the police and Sandy and her friends tomorrow, after everyone had gotten a good night's sleep. Peter Mullens agreed, and began to speak.

"Well, you've figured out that the newspaper clues were from an old code the gang used. That's how I knew they were meant for me, and that no one else would understand them. The first one threatened my wife and daughter, and then one last week asked me to meet the gang at the bank in Valley Village at midnight. The message said I wouldn't be harmed if I just brought the money. Now, for a while I had a suspicion that the gang believed I took some money from them when I left, which I didn't. I brought some financial documents with me to the meeting, hoping to prove to them that I didn't have any money. Well, they didn't believe me, and they kidnapped me. I overheard them talking about sending a ransom note to my wife, insinuating that I would be harmed if she didn't hand over the money. That was upsetting, because I knew there was no money and I knew Betty didn't have the ridiculous amount they were asking.

"After they sent the ransom note, though, I heard that the man they sent to watch the Connors household - where I gathered Betty was staying - had seen Sandy going to the police and they decided that the risk of picking up the ransom was too great so they didn't go. I think Becker really didn't believe that there was any stolen money anywhere; he was just hoping to get some money out of my wife or friends. Now, I gathered from what I overheard that the gang had mostly disbanded years ago, following the death of Clarence Becker, who was the leader back when I was a member. I guess these four members ran out of funds and were still looking for ways to get their hands on cash. They seemed pretty desperate for money.

"After the failed ransom note plot, the gang moved me from the abandoned cabin in the woods to the warehouse outside Santa Maria. I talked to my guard, Frank, who said the gang had been using both hideouts for several months, ever since they got on my trail to this area and they switched back and forth every few days. We should have gone back to the cabin in the woods a few days after that, but apparently one of the gang members saw some suspicious tire tracks on the dirt lane leading to it and Becker decided that it was too risky since the police were on to us. I happened to leave my shoes there and thought it was possible that someone had found them. I shall be glad to have the shoes back, because after I lost them I was given this pair to wear, and they are very ill fitting!" Peter Mullens held his leg up over the edge of the table and the group laughed to see him in a large, scuffed work boot, which was laced tightly to keep it from falling off.

"I guess that's about everything that happened. I will be glad to tell the story from the beginning tomorrow, but right now I would like to get some sleep without worrying about my own life, or my wife's and daughter's lives," Peter Mullens finished. Sandy said he could stay at her house, adding that Lisa's things were there already. Officer Murray agreed, asking the group to return in the morning, and soon the five were on the way back to Sandy's house for the night.

Sandy dropped Rose and Lily off at the Pinkerton's house, asking that they come over for breakfast the next morning. "We'll eat later; how does around 9:30 sound?" Sandy wanted the girls to be at her house for the remaining explanation of the kidnapping, and also to discuss the final step in solving the mystery. Rose and Lily said they would be there; adding that they could easily walk the blocks for the early spring weather had turned sunny and mild. Sandy then drove on to her house. Mr. and Mrs. Connors were pleased to meet Peter Mullens at last, and introductions were soon completed. Peter told a short version of his kidnapping and rescue, and then said "I hope you don't think me terribly rude, but it has been a long, trying day. I would be happy to tell the rest of my story tomorrow, but right now all I really want to do is rest. I'm so sorry."

"Oh, of course!" Mrs. Connors said, instantly apologetic for keeping the man up so late after his ordeal. She immediately showed him upstairs; adding that the guest room was small but as it was where his wife and daughter were sleeping she thought it would be most comfortable for him. She put an extra towel and pillow out while Mr. Connors brought the man a spare bathrobe and set of clothes to wear the next day. "We look about the same size," the older man said, "though my pants might be a bit short on you!" Peter Mullens thanked Sandy's father, saying that he appreciated the kindness and the fit of the pants would not bother him. With a few more words of thanks, Peter and Betty Mullens retired into the guest bedroom for the night.

Sandy, meanwhile, went back downstairs and, over a final cup of tea, told her parents the pieces of the story that Peter Mullens had left out in his brief narration. She also explained to her father about the car crash, for he had been at work when that occurred and had not heard the full story yet. The whole family knew about the police chase from the warehouse that had been featured on the evening news. She mentioned that she had asked Rose and Lily to come over the next morning for breakfast, to hear the beginning of the story and also to discuss the final piece of the mystery to be solved. "Final piece of the mystery!" Mrs. Connors exclaimed, "What else is there to solve?"

"The mystery of the missing $200,000!" Sandy said. "Peter Mullens say he does not have it, and I believe him, but neither Becker nor any of his gang members had it, either. So where is it? I think that the other men who fled the gang at the same time Peter Mullens - the Kent brothers - took it and somehow lost it, but I want to find out for certain. They passed away in Florida some years ago, both apparently penniless and mentally ill. In cases like that, someone is usually assigned as a financial guardian for an individual and I wonder who was acting as guardian for the Kents, and if that person might know about any large sums of money they lost. I would also like to see if the police accountants can make any more sense of the myriad bank statements we found in Becker's first car - and if the papers in the recently crashed brown coupe add any information. If the money in those accounts was taken from the gang's robbery hauls, then if could possibly be traced back to the banks where it was stolen and some of it returned to the people who lost it in the first place."

"That's a tall order, Sandy," Mr. Connors said. "Those robberies were committed, some of them, twenty years ago. And the leader of the gang for most of that time has passed away. I doubt that much of the money can be traced back to the banks or specific people from which it was stolen. Also, court appointed financial guardians are usually bound to secrecy and might not be able to talk about any of the Kent's financial information."

"I know it's a chance," Sandy said, "but I can't help feeling that if the people who were stolen from have any possibility of regaining any of their money, they should be helped. I want to go over the papers that I saw in the back of the brown coupe when it crashed and see if those are of any help in finding out where the money came from and where it should be returned. I think I will ask Officer Murray if he can be in touch with the police in Florida and ask them to search for any information about the Kents' financial situation since it's recently become relevant again, as a motive for this kidnapping. Perhaps the guardian himself would step forward in response to a little searching."

"I applaud the impulse, dear, but those are challenging undertakings. You shouldn't be too upset if you fail," Mrs. Connors cautioned her daughter. Sandy nodded and smiled but said that she was determined to try nevertheless. The small family chatted a few minutes longer about her attempt to retrace the path of the stolen money, then washed their teacups and went to bed.

The next morning, Sandy was awake early. She breakfasted with her father, who had to go to work that morning, and then began to cook brunch for the Mullens and the Pinkerton sisters. Her mother came down soon and the two women put together a meal of freshly baked coffee cake, fruit salad and hot tea. Shortly before 9:30, Peter and Betty came down with Lisa in tow, holding tightly to her father's hand as she watched her mother heat up milk and put it into a bottle for her. The couple greeted Sandy and Mrs. Connors and "Good mornings" were exchanged. Betty was settled down with Lisa in a dining room chair when the doorbell rang and the Pinkertons arrived, some minutes ahead of schedule. "Sorry to be early, Sandy, but we couldn't stay away! What an exciting day yesterday was!" Rose exclaimed. Sandy smiled and said the girls were welcome anytime. "We've got breakfast almost ready; if you girls will help set the table we can eat in just a few minutes!" Both sisters agreed to help and soon had the plates, cups and silver laid around the table. Peter and Betty greeted the sisters and within a few minutes the whole group was seated around the spacious dining room table, eating the prepared food.

Sandy said she felt they were not quite finished with solving this mystery. She first explained what she wanted to achieve by going through the financial documents one more time and looking at the papers that were left in the brown coupe to try to return the money to those from whom it had been stolen. She then mentioned the missing $200,000 and said she hoped to find out for certain whether or not the Kent brothers had taken it, and if so, what happened to it.

"Peter, you don't have any of that money hidden away anywhere, do you?" she asked. "I'm sorry to have to ask so bluntly, but if you have it, then there's no point in my asking the police to track down the Kent's financial guardian."

"No, I didn't take any money other than my take when I left the gang," Peter said. "I also didn't know that the Kent brothers were leaving the same day I did - that was pure coincidence - but I wouldn't be surprised if they took the money. Charlie Kent in particular was a nervous fellow all the time, but he seemed especially nervous the few days before we all ran off. I thought he was just nervous because he was planning to get away, but he might have been jittery because he was planning to steal money from Clarence Becker."

"How could he have stolen that money?" Sandy asked.

"Becker - Clarence, that is - had a notebook where he kept track of all of his accounts and dealings. All the amounts and numbers were in there. If one of the Kents got their hands on that notebook for a few minutes, it would have been enough time to take down a number or two and have access to that money. Becker guarded that notebook with his life, I will tell you that," Peter added with a shake of his head. Sandy was elated by this information.

"A notebook, you say. What happened to this notebook once Clarence Becker died?" She asked.

"I have to say I don't know," Peter said. "I would guess that his son, Jonas Becker, inherited it, along with all the other documents from the thefts. Clarence Becker kept immaculate records, and also did a very good job guarding them from prying eyes. If those records still exist, you could almost trace all the money and return it to the original owners!"

CHAPTER 37

"**O**h, I hope we're able to find that notebook!" Sandy said. "That might tell us all that we need to know about where the money came from and how to return it! Maybe this notebook is with the papers and files that were in the back of the brown car!" Sandy said that she would phone Officer Murray later that morning and ask when they could go and look at the files from the car.

"The sooner the better, it seems to me," Rose interjected, adding that any people who could be reimbursed for the thefts twenty years ago might be getting elderly now. "Some of them might even have passed away!" she said. Sandy admitted that this was true, but said she hoped many of them would still be alive or that they would have left wills which specified heirs who could be given the money. Peter Mullens said he had nothing more to add to the story of his kidnapping and release. Sandy asked him if he had any questions about how things happened in his absence, and he said he did not. They then finished breakfast and quickly washed and dried the dishes.

Sandy excused herself, saying she would phone the police station. Fortunately, she was able to reach Officer Murray, who said that the girls could come to the station at any point and look through the files. "We've taken everything out of the car; the car itself is totaled and will be removed to an impound lot later this week. Our men went over it thoroughly, though, so I'm sure there's nothing still in there." Sandy thanked the man and said that she would be down to the station soon. "We've gotten a clue about what to look for from Peter Mullens. May he come along with us to look through the documents?"

"By all means, bring him along. I hope he's feeling better after his release yesterday." Sandy thanked the officer and assured him that Peter was entirely recovered. She then said goodbye, promising to come soon to examine the paperwork. Going into the kitchen where the rest of the group was just finishing dishes, Sandy shared her plan. "I think Rose, Lily, Peter and I should go to the station. Betty, if you feel okay staying here, it would really be easier for Lisa not to come. We might be looking through papers for a good while and she would get bored. We will look for this notebook Peter mentioned, or anything else that will show us where the money is being stored, and where it came from. If we can determine how to get it back to the people who originally had it stolen from them, all the better."

The group agreed, and soon the foursome was on the way to the police station. Sandy asked the group to examine closely any notebooks they found. Everyone agreed, and soon they had reached the station. Sandy pulled into the parking lot and the small group went inside. The receptionist showed them immediately into the conference room. Officer Murray came in with a large box full of papers shortly after the group arrived. Sandy recognized some of them from the first set that the group had gone through. He dumped the box out in the middle of the table and they soon were paging through the piles.

There was silence for several minutes, until Sandy recalled the other goal. "Officer Murray," she asked, "is there any way that someone from this station could get in touch with the police in Florida where the

Kent brothers died to see if there's record of any large sums of money held, then lost by them?" She briefly explained about trying to trace the missing $200,000, and her theory that the Kents took it but then lost it before they were taken to the mental facilities where they passed. Officer Murray agreed, saying that he would send an inquiry to the Florida State Police. "Of course, sometimes financial records are sealed, but since the individuals in this case are deceased - and they both passed away while in US custody in mental institutions - the information might be available."

Officer Murray left to send the inquiry to the Florida Police and the group continued sorting.

Again, there was silence for several minutes; the only sounds were pages turning and being cast aside. Presently, Lily heaved a sigh. "These records are so mixed up. I don't know if even with the notebook which explains everything would we be able to make sense of them!" Peter Mullens agreed that the records were a mess, adding that Jonas Becker seemed to have been a less organized individual than his father. "Perhaps all the information for which we're searching is here, though, if we can just make sense of it." Several more minutes passed, and Sandy had almost despaired of finding the notebook - the group had been through almost the whole stack of papers without any trace of a single one - when Lily suddenly yelled in triumph. She was holding up a small, red leather notebook.

"Peter, is that the notebook?" Sandy asked.

"I think so - let me see it, please," the man asked. Lily handed the small document to him, and he opened the first page. "Property of Clarence Becker, Private," he read out loud. "This certainly looks like the same notebook." He began to flip through pages and read a few of the notations aloud. "December third, 1938; twenty-three thousand from Allied Bank, Chicago; accounts 12678809, 12678810, 12678811. There are dozens more like that in here!"

"This is exactly what I had hoped to find!" Sandy said, elated that her hunch had proved to be correct. "We can use the rest of these papers and match them to the notations in that book and we should be able to return much of the money to the people who originally earned it. Rose, aren't some of those papers you have current account statements?" The younger girl nodded, pushing a pile of papers over to Sandy. Sandy looked through them, then said, "It might take several hours of sorting and organizing, but it looks like there's several hundred thousand dollars worth of money in these accounts, when all combined. If we can divide that evenly amongst the people who were stolen from, we should be able to return much of the money."

"And what about the $200,000?" Peter asked. "Do you think you'll be able to find and return that?"

"Perhaps not," Sandy conceded. "If the Kent brothers did take it, and spent it all, we won't be able to get that back. But these amounts should be able to be returned, and that might help out any number of these families!" At that moment, Officer Murray returned, saying that he had been in contact with an officer from the Florida State Police.

"He will do what he can to find out about the Kent brothers' financial situation. There's no guarantee that we will discover anything, but if they did have a large sum and lost it we might be able to find that out. How is the search for the notebook going?" He asked. In response, Sandy held up the small book and grinned. "We still have several hours of organizing to do, but we should be able to find out where most of the money was taken from and return much of it to the original owners!"

"Congratulations, Sandy," the officer said. "This was a good piece of detective work!"

"The families certainly should congratulate you also," Rose said, "when they get back a sum of money that was stolen from them fifteen or twenty years ago! In Chicago there will be a parade in your honor!"

Sandy just smiled.

Three weeks later, Sandy was again hosting the Mullens at her house for dinner. She also invited Rose and Lily Pinkerton. She and her mother prepared roast beef and mashed potatoes. Sandy had collected a pile of letters she now set in the middle of the dining room table. The letters were postmarked primarily from the Chicago area, but one she placed at the top of the pile was postmarked from a small town in central Florida. Sandy set the table and helped her mother put the final touches on the meal. Presently the bell rang and Sandy went to the door. Peter and Betty Mullens arrived, with Lisa toddling along beside. Sandy ushered them inside and showed them to the dining room.

"Look at little Lisa! When did she start walking?" Mrs. Connors asked when the little family had reached the kitchen. The older woman handed the child a small toy she had saved for her and was rewarded with a shy smile. Sandy showed them their seats, including a special high chair her family had set up for Lisa. She had refused to tell those assembled why she asked them for dinner, and now she merely smiled and said there were several more guests still to arrive before she could share what was going on. Betty Mullens looked around at the table and counted the place settings.

"Don't tell me; I think I can guess for whom we're waiting! Could it perhaps be Rose and Lily Pinkerton?" Sandy conceded that she was right, adding that she wanted to tell the whole group about how the mystery had been resolved. "I have several letters here I want you all to read; they all contain good news!" Betty, who looked happier and healthier than Sandy had seen her before, again thanked the young sleuth.

"I'm glad you were able to return much of the money, but I will never forget how your solving this mystery returned my husband to me and took my child out of danger." The woman, who had tears welling in her eyes, looked at Sandy, who responded graciously. At that moment the doorbell rang. Sandy excused herself and went to answer the door. Betty Mullens, glad of the opportunity to collect her thoughts took Lisa into the kitchen to speak with Mrs. Connors. The two women chatted about raising children while they overheard Sandy greeting the Pinkerton sisters at the front door.

Sandy opened the door and ushered the two girls inside. She said that the other guests had already arrived and dinner would soon be served. The sisters went into the dining room and greetings were exchanged. A few moments later, Mrs. Connors said that the roast was ready. "Please take your seats, everyone. I will be bringing the roast to carve," Mrs. Connors said. The group immediately sat down at the places indicated for them with handmade place cards. Betty was pleased to note that Lisa's place was set between herself and her husband.

Soon Mrs. Connors came in with a steaming, delicious-looking roast. She placed it on the sideboard and carved generous slices for each member of the group. Sandy served mashed potatoes from a china dish and a bowl of fresh salad was passed around the table. As soon as everyone had been served, Sandy took her place at the table. Mrs.

Connors was seated next to her daughter and she, too, took her chair. Mrs. Connors said a short grace, adding her thanks that everyone was able to attend the dinner safely and for the successful conclusion to the mystery. After her guests began to eat, Sandy took the small pile of letters from where it sat in the center of the table and began to pass them around. She saved the one with the Florida postmark for herself.

"These letters are from people who received money in the reimbursement process after the capture of the criminals. Please feel free to read them, and pass them around so everyone can read them all," she said.

"Sandy, what's in the letter you've saved right there?" Peter Mullens asked.

"I'm going to read this one last," Sandy said, smiling enigmatically. "It explains another small part of the mystery that hadn't yet been solved." She waved her hands at her friends, saying "Please, eat the roast before it gets cold! And read the letters, too. Feel free to read and eat at the same time!"

Rose Pinkerton declared that she was capable of reading and eating at the same time, and she was the first to open her letter while also taking a bite of the succulent roast. The young girl declared the roast to be stupendous and thanked the Connors for providing the delicious repast. Lily, smiling at her sister said "And for all that, you've become distracted from your reading! And here you said you were good at doing both!" She also opened her letter and began to read as she took a forkful of mashed potatoes. She was forced to admit that reading and eating at the same time was a more difficult undertaking than she had heretofore recognized, as she dropped her letter into her plate of food while chewing. With an exclamation, she pulled it out, noting abashedly the gravy dripping off of the back.

"Well, this idea didn't turn out as I had planned!" Sandy said, laughing gaily at the chaos. "Here, Lily, let me get a paper towel for that and I will set it in the kitchen to dry." She got the paper towels and took the sodden missive from her friend's hands. Rose teased her sister about her empty boasts and said, "at least I didn't drop mine into my food!" When Sandy returned from the kitchen she suggested a new plan.

"Why don't I tell you all about what happened and what these letters say, and then once we've cleared the plates you all can read them for yourselves? They all agreed to this new plan, and Sandy explained how she and Officer Murray went through the papers and notebook and matched all the notations to the bank statements taken from Becker's cars.

"It was a painstaking process; we first had to determine which papers were current bank statements and credit card bills and which were papers from old accounts, old bills and other out of date things. It took an afternoon, but we were able to determine that, even after paying Becker's outstanding debts, of which there were many, he still had approximately half a million dollars in all his accounts, of which there were myriad."

Rose and Lily gasped at hearing that number. Peter Mullens looked grim, and Betty appeared surprised at the magnitude of the thefts. "How much was stolen by the gang, throughout their entire working span?" she asked.

"To find that out, we had to go through Clarence Becker's notebook. You all saw this notebook - it was a small book, but each page was filled up with notations, and each notation took up two to three lines at most. He wrote a notation for each robbery, as well as notes of accounts opened for the gang's ill-gained money, payments of bills on credit cards opened, members joining, leaving or passing away. We went through that notebook and found that, in total, the gang had stolen nearly two million dollars throughout the twenty years they were in business." Here the entire table gasped; even Peter Mullens looked surprised.

"Two million! I had no idea so much was taken!" he said, looking shocked. Sandy reassured him that he was not being held culpable for any of the thefts, and had, in fact, been completely exonerated. "We went through all the records and found that this was the case. We also found notes of monies given to members of the gang following each robbery, and it looks like Clarence Becker kept the largest part of each sum for himself. He opened up many accounts to hide the money and keep people from suspecting how wealthy he was. Most of this money went to Jonas Becker following Clarence's death.

"Jonas was not nearly as meticulous at record keeping as his father had been, and that's when the gang began to lose steam. Jonas still noted all of his personal financial assets, but he did not always keep track of where money was stolen from or how much went to each gang member. Finally, a few pages after the note saying that Peter Simpson and Charles and Parker Kent had run off, taking $200,000 from a specific account, the notations end. Officer Murray said that the time the notations in the notebook end corresponds to the time when the bank robberies cease, so we are assuming that the gang stopped work at that point." Sandy paused to eat some of her roast beef. She looked around the table and was surprised to see everyone staring open mouthed at her.

"Sandy, that's incredible!" Rose said. "Do you mean that by going through that notebook you were able to find out all that, and match the stolen money to the people from whom it had been taken?" Sandy laughed at the disbelief in her friend's voice.

"Well, we had a few more steps to accomplish first. We got records from the banks in Chicago that had thefts around that time; Officer Murray was able to get them even though they are confidential, because he's a police officer and had a current case directly relevant to the old thefts; and we worked on matching up account numbers. We didn't have any names - the notebook kept only names of the gang members, not the victims, and the bank records did not have names attached, for security's sake. We were able to match up about eighty percent of the current accounts to numbers that were in the notebook. Officer Murray corresponded with the banks' presidents, and we determined that, of those accounts, nearly all had been open twenty years ago, so we assumed that the same people, or direct descendants of those people, were still the account holders.

"This left us with a total of one hundred twenty one accounts which we were planning to reimburse. We thought about setting up a sliding scale, and giving more money back to the people who had had more stolen from the accounts originally, but since we were not able to determine with certainty that the same people owned the accounts currently, we decided that was not the best idea. So instead we divided the remainder of the money up between all the accounts, and with the cooperation of the Chicago police department and presidents of these various banks, we issued money transfers to those accounts. The owners of the accounts were informed by registered letter of what the money was and from where it came, and that is how we solved the final portion of the mystery!"

The group around the table began to clap and Rose whistled loudly. Sandy, who disliked scenes in her honor, waved off the attention and asked everyone to continue eating. "After we finish eating, we'll go into the other room and read through some of the letters and see what some of the people have said, along with this letter from Florida which clears up the final portion of the mystery," Sandy said, pulling the letter out from under her plate.

"Florida!" Rose said, suddenly making the connection. "Is that about the Kent brothers, who supposedly took a large sum of money?"

"Yes, Rose, it is. I'll read portions of it to you all," Sandy said, unfolding the letter carefully. It was a long letter and Sandy showed the group paragraphs that she had underlined which related to the case at hand. "This letter was sent to Officer Murray, from a policeman in Florida who had investigated charges of financial fraud levied against one Parker Kent only a few months before his death. The case was eventually dropped because Parker Kent was mentally unstable. He died, penniless, in a state hospital shortly after the case was dropped. The officer looked into Kent's past following the original charges and found that he and his brother, who was also in a mental hospital, had recently made large donations to a youth baseball league in southern Florida. The total of these donations, which were made over a period of a few months, added up to nearly $200,000.

"The officer went to speak to Charles Kent, who was not indicted on the original charges of fraud, which incidentally had the wrong Kent brothers all along. The officer found that, though Charles Kent was quite mentally unstable and barely capable of speaking clearly, he did remember some things about a past in Chicago and spoke several times about a "Redman" and robbing banks. The officer, who at the time did not understand what the "Redman" reference meant, said that he is now certain that those Kent brothers were the ones who left the gang twenty years ago, and the $200,000 they donated to a youth baseball league was the stolen money. Apparently, as their mental states declined, they made the donations out of some sense of logic which is not apparent to anyone else."

Sandy sighed as she finished telling her tale, taking another bite of her food. She saw that everyone around her was almost done eating while she had barely begun! "Lily, why don't you read some of those letter aloud to people, now that you're finished eating, while I eat my roast?" She requested. With a smile, Lily agreed and was soon reading the missives, all of which thanked Sandy and her friends for helping to return the long-missing money. Several spoke eloquently about how the money would be helpful for repairing a house or sending a child to school. The whole group listened, rapt, to the letters, but Sandy found that her attention began to wander. Would she ever again solve such a fascinating and challenging mystery? she wondered. Lily noticed her friend's wandering attention but did not say anything. She knew Sandy well enough to know that she was already thinking ahead to new mysteries, and hoping that an interesting one would come her way soon!

THE END

233

Stephanie Rosenbaum lives in Carmel Valley, CA. She is currently studying at the Monterey Institute of International Studies, pursuing a dual masters degree in Public Administration and International Education Management. She is an active volunteer with the Monterey Bay Aquarium and the SPCA of Monterey County. She enjoys traveling, reading, writing, cooking and spending time with her two dogs, Snuffy and China. This is her second novel.

Thanks and Acknowledgements:

My deepest gratitude goes to friends and family who helped and supported me through the process of writing and editing this novel. Sandy and Art Schuller, Rick Rosenbaum, Jenny Rosenbaum and Daisy Davis - thank you for reading countless drafts and lending your editing and revising genius.

Ginna and David Gordon - you are miracle workers, and I am deeply grateful to be able to work with you at Lucky Valley Press.

Carmel, California
luckyvalleypress.com

Text: Optima
Display: Copperplate

Wood products used in the manufacture of this book meet the
Sustainable Forestry Initiative® Chain-of-Custody Standards.

www.sfiprogram.org